Hawks

&

Other Stories

Peter Hollywood

D1344333

NEW ISLAND

HAWKS
First published 2013
by New Island
2 Brookside
Dundrum Road
Dublin 14

www.newisland.ie

PRINT ISBN: 978-1-84840-236-2
EPUB ISBN: 978-1-84840-237-9
MOBI ISBN: 978-1-84840-238-6

British Library Cataloguing Data. A CIP catalogue record for
this book is available from the British Library

Typeset by JM InfoTech INDIA
Cover design by Andrew Brown
Printed by TJ International Ltd, Padstow, Cornwall

New Island received financial assistance from
The Arts Council (An Comhairle Ealaíon), Dublin, Ireland

10 9 8 7 6 5 4 3 2 1

To Michael and Brian – the brothers.

About The Author

Peter Hollywood was born in Newry at the tail-end of 1959 and began writing at an early age. Hollywood is married with three children who are erroneously convinced that they are the models for the siblings in the stalked and harassed family at the centre of his first novel. Having worked in a wide range of jobs, Hollywood currently plies his trade in the field of education and literacy.

Also By Peter Hollywood

Jane Alley

Lead City And Other Stories

Luggage

Contents

'Thinking is a dizzy business.'

– *Dashiell Hammett*

Farrow and Ball

For J M

The first occasion they came into the shop, they took four cans of Farrow and Ball black paint.

The following night, the police found two local girls bound to lamp-posts with their heads half shaved. Black paint had been poured over them and then the feathers from some gutted pillows. In those days not many people had heard of synthetic material.

After this event, Sergeant Ferris came into the shop for the first time. Declan's father had been in the office at the back and came out now at the sound of the spring-action bell that alerted him to any entrance to or exit from his premises. He eyed the empty can the policeman carried; there was a black tongue of paint lolled down its side. Behind the massive bulk of the sergeant, his father saw the police Land Rover taking up the kerb space reserved for the shop's delivery van. Declan was off school and his father had sent him to the wholesalers to pick up stock.

— Are you the key-holder? Ferris enquired.

— I am indeed.

— Mr Flood is it?

— Me again, his father confirmed.

The sergeant raised the can up into full view.

— Do you stock this brand?

Declan's father indicated a pyramidal display of similar cans over to the side of the shop.

— Do you know if you've sold any over the past day or two?

— Not sold, his father said. I've had four cans taken.

— You mean shop-lifted? Ferris looked amazed.

— No. Taken. Two young lads came in and told me they were taking them. That's all.

— What age were they?

— Well. My son's eighteen. They would've been a little older, I guess.

Ferris was silent a while as he considered this information. At length he looked at Declan's father and asked:

— Would you recognise them again?

Mr Flood shrugged his shoulders.

— They were just young fellas. Like any others.

The sergeant digested this response as he gazed at the can still in his hand. Then he came forward and placed

the can in the middle of the counter between him and
Mr Flood.

   — Did you report the theft?

   — What was the point? For a couple of cans of
paint. I will if it happens again, he assured the policeman.

Ferris seemed to be in the habit of taking his time,
weighing up information, deciding on his next comment or response. Eventually he made up his mind
and turned slowly to leave the shop.

   — Do, he advised over his shoulder as he opened
the door, glanced up at the bell and stepped out into
the street, scrutinising the roof-tops opposite as he
went.

From his position behind the counter, Mr Flood could
not count how many police officers had accompanied
Ferris, but there was a lot of noise and commotion as
they remounted into the back of the Land Rover and
drove away.

   — We want the keys to the van, one of two new
youths said the second time.

Declan's father objected:

   — Jesus, lads. I need the van for my business. You
can't take it.

   — We've orders to take it.

As Declan's father handed over the keys he asked:

    — Will I get the van back?

    — You're not to report it missing for six hours, was the sole reply he got to his anxious enquiry.

Sergeant Ferris rang him in the middle of the night to tell him the van had been reported abandoned in the middle of an estate in the north of the city; it was undamaged and the keys were in the ignition. His father roused Declan out of bed, despite the fact that he had been burning the midnight oil revising for an examination the next day. He drove his father in the family car to retrieve the van. They must have been moving munitions for the petrol tank was near empty and the floor of the van was littered with cigarette butts.

A month later they came and took the van again.

    — Did they threaten you? Sergeant Ferris wanted to know.

    He was flanked by a constable who was studiously taking notes. The two men seemed to fill up the shop floor on the customer side of the counter. On the other side stood Mr Flood and behind him, standing in the doorway of the office, Declan looked on.

    — Yes. Of course they did.

Ferris looked sideways waiting for his colleague to scribble this response.

— I'll need a copy of the police report for the insurance, his father informed the officers. This time the van had been found burnt out.

— And they definitely threatened you? Ferris pressed the point.

Mr Flood locked eyes with the sergeant. The note-taker looked up at the sudden silence.

— Yes. They said the shop would go up if I didn't do what they asked, Declan's father slowly and firmly impressed upon them.

The insurance paid for a replacement van and it was six months before they came for this one.

— For fuck sake, boys. I've only just got her. After the last time.

— It's orders, mister, one of them said, holding out his hand for the keys.

They got this van back but with a good deal of damage done to the body work due to it having rammed a police road-block. The van had then mounted a traffic island and the occupants had run off into the night.

On this occasion, Ferris had a new line of enquiry.

— Did they have a gun when they came to take the van?

— A gun? Mr Flood looked askance at the sergeant. They could have, I suppose.

— But you didn't see one, Ferris confirmed.

— Why? What are you saying? Mr Flood suddenly demanded.

— It's just I hear the insurance people are beginning to look for details like that. They're out a fortune with high-jackings and car-bombs and joy riders. You can imagine.

— And I'm out a fortune paying their premiums.

— Well. I'm sure it'll not be a problem this time. We'll fax through a copy of the report, Ferris said, turning to leave and looking out and up at the rooftops opposite.

Mr Flood didn't recognise the two youths running across traffic towards the shop but he guessed their intent. The plumper of the two approached the counter while his accomplice lingered like a look-out at the door.

— We want your van, he announced.

— Do you have a gun? Declan's father enquired of him. This wrong-footed the youth.

— What? He said as if he couldn't quite believe his ears.

— You must have a gun, Mr Flood advised him.

At a loss, the youth looked around as if appealing for assistance from his partner at the door but he just looked nervous and on edge. The youth stood a few moments, eyeing Declan's father all the while, weighing up the situation; then, he turned on his heel and, signalling to his companion by jerking his head in the direction of the street, left the shop and ran back again across the traffic.

It was after lunch when the same pair re-appeared. Coming forward but glancing backwards out at the street, the fat one opened the flap of his denim jacket. There was a gun stuck in the waist-band of his jeans. Declan's father turned and went into the little back office to get the keys.

— Yes. They had a gun, Mr Flood assured Sergeant Ferris. Both of them watched as the constable noted this down; then, from Ferris:

— Did he produce it?

— What?

— Did the youth take it out and physically threaten you with it, Ferris rephrased the question.

— Are you joking me or what? Declan's father eyeballed the sergeant. Is this the next thing?

— I'm just saying it's a wonder the insurance people haven't been asking questions; that's all.

The final occasion they came into the shop was on a Saturday because Declan's sister was working with them behind the counter. The one with the gun wore a khaki-coloured bush hat pulled low over his eyes. Although he had not been in the shop before, he went through the motions of opening the front of his Wrangler jacket to show the shop-keeper that he was armed. At the same time he recited his line, requesting the keys of the van.

    — No, Declan's father simply said. Fuck off out of my shop.

The youth pushed up the brim of his hat, the better to get a look at the older man. Declan and his sister looked at their father too. When they looked back at the youth they could see his face contorted with the effort of coming up with the appropriate verbal response. Eventually, unable to compose one, he drew the gun and waved it about for a moment for all to see, then suddenly aimed it straight at Mr Flood's head.

    — The keys, he shouted. Now.

The older man's reflexes took them all by surprise. His right hand shot up and gripped the barrel of the gun. He did not do this to deflect the gun away from him. Instead he pressed the muzzle more firmly against the side of his head and half-whispered to the youth to pull the trigger.

    — Go on, he urged him. You people are fucking bleeding me dry. I can't make ends meet. The insurance people are going to refuse to pay out any more. You won't leave me alone even though I've been serving this community for over twenty years. I'm slowly but surely going under. Go on: shoot.

Frantically, the youth tried to pull his gun away.

— Let go of my fucking gun, will you, he shouted.

Pulling with all his might, the gun came free suddenly and the youth stumbled backwards, almost toppling a stand of paint brushes, white spirit and masking tape in the process.

— Fuck, he roared at no-one in particular while looking wildly around him. Then seeing Declan he grabbed him by the neck and stuck the gun up against his head instead, the barrel half disappearing into the depths of his thick, Rory Gallagher head of long hair. Declan's sister started to cry. The youth looked at Declan's father to make sure he got the point.

— Him? Mr Flood exploded. Jesus. He's a liability. I'm going to have to pay three hundred pounds a month so that he can go to university. He's a drain. Go ahead. You'd be doing me a favour.

Declan had a close-up, almost magnified view of the startled expression on the youth's face and for the stillest of moments, the youth turned his head away from the direction of his father and their eyes met. Then, before he fled from the shop, he said:

— You're fucking mad, mister, you are. You need your head looking at.

The spring-action bell seemed to ring longer than normal in the silence that ensued. Then Declan's sister burst out crying again.

— Stop your crying, girl, her father said.

The old man moved and went back into the little office behind the counter. The keys to the van were still hanging from the hook on the wall below a framed black and white photograph of Mohammad Ali; it was taken at a training camp for Ali who seemed suspended in mid-air, surrounded by the thin smoke of a skipping rope. If you looked closely you could just make out Angelo Dundee watching paternally from the sidelines.

When Declan went to the door of the office, his father was sitting at the desk. Its surface was a clutter of bills, invoices, and order forms. He was staring blankly at the pile of paperwork and Declan stood in the doorway waiting for his father to look up at him. At length, his father spoke but he did not look up at him.

— Go on, son, he said. Go on out there and mind the shop.

After the Conflict

After the conflict, huge, mechanical cranes suddenly overarched the city centre sky line and skips appeared in the suburbs.

Property prices soared, after the conflict, and most people stopped moving house. Instead, they renovated; there were loft conversions and kitchen extensions; front gardens were often slabbed over, gravelled or interred in tar macadam to make secure parking space for one or both cars. There were hagglings and horse-tradings with architects and surveyors, negotiations with planning services; tenders sought from small construction companies, whose small, dirty vans were seen buzzing about everywhere. Loans arranged; re-mortgagings. Lawyers and barristers managed to move house. Elsewhere there were rows over boundary lines and deeds produced from nowhere; cans of white spray X-ing driveways and walls with what looked like badly applied band-aids.

After the conflict, you could hardly get a plumber or plasterer for love or money; some brave souls had a go at it themselves.

In the suburbs there were Kangos and Bobcats and long lorries, loaded with red brick and breeze blocks, Rosemary tiles or Bangor Blues; setts and cobbles: Cedar, Heather, Charcoal and Bracken; Old Court flags or textured and riven flags, Sandstone circular and kerbsetts: Autumn Brown, Sage Green, Sahara. There was traffic congestion in small avenues and closes, courts and cul de sacs.

Daylight burst down, Bible-like, after the conflict, through apertures in roofs made for the insertion of Vellux skylights and dark and dust scurried off on four legs and eight for cover under the suddenly exposed joists, purlins and rafters. Wasp-nests were detonated, swallows and swifts and bats put to flight.

Avenues clanged with the sound of industry. Little corner shops did a brief boom trade in cigarettes and sandwiches, high energy drinks and newspapers, Mars bars and teabags. Urban foxes poked their noses into suddenly overloaded yellow skips. Dog-walkers strolled past and peered inquisitively into the rash of miniature building sites, taking notes, inspecting, making comparisons and simply satisfying their own curiosity. On dry, windy days, there were mini sand-storms and tarpaulins flapped and slapped loudly; plastic carry-out coffee cups and torn plastic sheets, fangs of white polystyrene got ensnared in people's hedges and neighbours complained about the mess the street was in and the health and safety impli-cations of badly illuminated skips at night. People peered out through double glazing, conservatories. Orangeries.

All the time, downtown, the construction contin-ued apace. Old buildings that had survived the conflict got make-overs and face-lifts or were torn down and demolished; making way for the new. CCTV sniffed the air.

Meanwhile, a smarter class of helicopter began to buzz the skies above us, lighter and brightly bubbled and often with a corporate logo emblazoned on the fuselage. Police cars too became candied and colour-ful. Helmets and flap-jackets were mostly shed. For a brief season, youths purchased pink and lilac kaki coloured combats from high street stores.

Talk of betrayal began to fade from beer-soaked, heated bar-room debate replaced instead with words such as amnesty and reconciliation; the obfuscating fug of cigarette smoke lifted too with that ban. According to some critics and commentators, however, it was not cool to write about the conflict any more, preferring that authors did not dwell overmuch on the Troubles.

So, from Canada and America came ice-hockey players; plasterers and plumbers from Eastern Europe, furniture from Sweden. Then, also from America, sub-prime mortgages became a topic of vexed conversa-tion along with the associated fear of a credit crunch so that property prices took a tumble and people con-tinued to mostly stop moving house. In flood-plains wise residents moved sockets higher up their walls and demanded more regular purgation of drains. Many retained sodden sand-bags; just in case. There was talk of climate change.

However, out in the countryside, someone was setting age-old Orange Halls alight and hoax devices were being found tethered to railings around rural Gaelic playing fields. It appeared dark men were still meeting in late places.

Yet the people are resilient; it is after the conflict now and they renovate and home-improve, extend, redecorate and all the time appreciate the city and its transformations; but every-so-often, in the midst of this flurry of activity, some might stop and look around them. Watch them. Periodically, they will pause and, for a moment, hesitate as if unsure of this normality. It might be the hawk shadow of a low-cost airplane passing overhead, or the hollow boom of an empty skip being clumsily dumped to the ground. It might simply be the lack of noise; silence.

Whatever, they will look around; then, when reassured, they'll proceed about their business.

The Spanish Civil War

The young couple the waiter served beers to on the terrasse of the hotel Los Piñades in Noja would break up shortly after returning home from their holiday.

They were polite to each other now and polite to the waiter when he set the dos cañas down between them on the table. The glasses beaded agreeably in the hot July sun. Sarah's friends kept texting her about how bad the weather was at home.

— Pity we didn't find this hotel first, Dan said for the terrasse overlooked the crowded beach and the view went on out to sea.

— Can't be helped, Sarah appealed. She had chosen their hotel, further along the shore-front. It was cheap but comfortable; some mornings they could hear the surf from beyond the sand-dunes opposite the hotel.

On the second day of the holiday, Dan had purchased a body-board in one of the surf shops. Goggles and swim-wear he had packed and taken with him. There were black clad surfers paddling and straddling their boards on the swell and after sitting beside Sarah a while, rubbing sun screen on her back and shoulders while watching their technique, he ran down to the sea. The life-guards from their high metal perch would have had little difficulty spotting his pale form splashing in and attempting to paddle out to join them. The rip-tide whipped him over to the rocks with such speed he had barely time to feel alarmed. Instead he tried to kick both himself and board back into the beach but was suspended in a state of flailing stasis; the beach tantalisingly just out of reach. Arching his head he saw two tanned youths running down to the water. Through goggle-fog he watched them stop briefly to snap on fluorescent green flippers, for they were the life guards coming to assist him.

— Tranquilo, they said to him, bobbing either side of him.

Sarah was in front of a small group of spectators as he emerged from the water.

— I'm alright, he insisted. I wasn't even in any great danger.

— I saw them running down and suddenly realised it was you. Are you sure you're okay?

— There ought to be a warning sign, he said.

— There is, she said pointing up the beach.

He left the board leaning up beside an ironing board in a small alcove behind reception in the hotel.

Early Sunday morning Sarah was roused from her sleep by him getting up for mass.

— You don't usually go at home. Do you? She enquired.

— I just want to see what a Spanish mass is like. It wouldn't do you any harm either to go to church.

— I doubt they have a Church of Ireland in the vicinity, she said, turning away from the light coming from the window through the white blinds.

He proceeded quietly to get ready and she heard him closing the door silently behind him when he left. Then she was astounded to find herself suddenly sexually aroused. She lay still, astonished. She replayed that article she had read in one of his men's magazines about how a hotel room could act as a powerful aphrodisiac; but it hadn't meant this. She saw the illustration that had accompanied the article and the two running lifeguards with their dark skin and long hair and, with a groan of resignation, rolled over onto her back. The white sunlight through the blind had grown brighter.

Dan was glad she had not wanted to accompany him. He planned to go for a quiet drink afterwards in one of the cafés in the square over from the church. The mass, however, depressed him. It was full of old people. Most of the men were neat and dapper in short-sleeved plaid shirts, nipped and tucked into stone or beige slacks with tan coloured belts and loafers to match. Some of the old women looked the part in traditional mantillas; others wore smart, expensive dress suits. Dan stayed long enough to feel that it was no longer an old religion but an old people's religion and then he left to have a drink.

It was like All-Ireland Day build-up on the plasma screen in the café across from the church. Dan stood at the counter and ordered a white wine. From there he watched what he realised was coverage of the opening day of the St. Fermin Feria in Pamplona. Hearty presenters tried to conduct outdoor broadcasts jostled by white clad revellers with knotted red scarves and boinas. Although he couldn't understand the Spanish commentary, he could easily make out the crowd's growing excitement in advance of that day's Encierro; the running of the bulls.

— What is it with the Spanish and bulls? He'd asked her, when at her suggestion they'd hired a car and driven to the museum and replica of the Altamira caves.

— It's obviously something ingrained in their psyche, she surmised. Something very ancient. She pointed out to him how the ancient artists had used the natural contours of the rock walls to give a three dimensional effect.

— Picasso, she told him. Said: 'After Altamira, all is decadence.'

He had been reluctant at first to make the drive into the Cantabrian mountains but looking up at the ancient drawings he was glad she had made him go; but he could not understand what she saw in the Juan Munoz installations in the Guggenheim, Bilbao. Or Meret Oppenheim's 'Table with bird's legs'; or Marcel Jean's 'Panels from a wardrobe'; Magritte's 'On the threshold of Liberty.' Leonor Fini's 'Corset chair' he quite liked. Half way through, he told her he had had enough and for her not to hurry; he'd go and have a beer and wait for her outside.

When she wandered out onto the large balcony to view Jeff Koon's entangled Tulips she spied him down on the bank of the River Nervion. (He had come upon the giant spider after having a quick beer in the outdoor café in the park adjacent to the museum.) He inexplicably pointed up at Louise Bourgeois' creation entitled 'Maman'. (Struck by its immense size and freakish appearance in the middle of the city, he checked around him and suddenly zapped the monster with an imaginary ray-gun before continuing his circuit around the outside of the building.) She was puzzled for from her vantage point there seemed to be no-one around him; then he wandered on.

Whatever about the exhibits within, he was really taken with the great tin-foil splash of the building in the sun and didn't mind waiting for her sitting there in the sunshine outside the Guggenheim. He watched all sorts of tourists come and go. Two pretty Japanese girls; a hippy couple; a family group, the young son of which ran and pretended to catch and support one of the Munoz falling figures, that lined the steps down to the atrium, and the father insisted on taking a snap. Dan hoped the digital camera would capture the visual jape. One of the oriental, sculpted figures sitting on a bench above his falling mate seemed to hug himself, and, with the rictus of a grin on his face, enjoy the joke.

They fell out about how best to get back to the underground car-park in Plaza Salgrado Corazón. They had attempted to go by metro but the little man in the ticket kiosk had refused to sell them tickets; instead, he did something that Dan had never witnessed before in a public transport network anywhere else on his travels: he got up from his seat and emerged from the security of his little ticket office to stand with them on the concourse and explain himself, though not before locking the office door behind him first.

— El Metro, no es lo mejor, the man tried to explain. Para este viaje. El Tranvia, he counselled; and, pausing, he looked quizzically at them. El Tranvia?

— Si. Tram: tranvia, Dan said to show he half-understood.

— El tranvia es mejor. The Metro man continued.

To further aid them, he consulted the tram route, tilting his head back to better regard the schedule and relaying information back to them unaware of their blank looks of incomprehension.

Thanking him, Dan walked out of the metro station with Sarah at his shoulder reminding him that they had no idea how to use the tram system.

— You should have insisted on getting a metro ticket.

— How come I've all of a sudden become the expert in Spanish? Dan wanted to know. Why didn't you insist?

— Well where the hell do you even go to get a tram? And what direction do we take? And: tickets? We'll be all hours, she complained.

— 'We' didn't have to do all that shopping in the old quarter and try on all those dresses, he reminded her. Before she could reply, they spotted a tram gliding past the Teatro Arriaga and ran to gauge where it would come to a stop.

There was a gathering of Bilbaon pensioners who were holding a demonstration, and placards and banners with legends and slogans daubed in Euskara. Nevertheless, some of the group came away from the main body and escorted Dan to the nearest ticket machine and pointed out the line-direction to go in and the stop at which to disembark; and the metro man was right in his counsel for the futuristic tram they rode eventually whispered to a stop a stone's throw from where they'd left the hire-car.

   — Panic over, Dan said as they drove out of the city.

The next day, he stayed by the pool and finished Ernie O'Malley's 'On Another Man's Wounds'; and she went to the beach with Eva Figes' 'Light' and her iPod. Now they sat with those beers between them on the table and there was a type of truce holding. They were on the eve of returning home.

From their vantage point, they took in together the sun-spangled spectacle of the beach stretching out beneath them; the wonderful mix and match of people. There was one man in baggy shorts standing in the sea with his hands behind his back. Children splashed in the shallows. Another, older man stood in shorter trunks with his folded arms resting on the huge convex of his belly, conversing with two elderly ladies lying on towels. More children rock-climbed. Two teenage girls stepped equestrian-like along the water's edge. Like golden chain-mail, sun scales covered the surface of the evening sea. A warm breeze blew. A surfer seemed melded with the molten water. The pepper pot of another Romanesque church stood on the mountain slope across the bay. A string bikini top was removed like the merest wisp of cigarette smoke. A kite shot up and down like an autograph. Children ran screaming around beneath it as it rose and dipped and banked and swooped down upon the people on the beach.

The young couple sat there on the terrasse of the hotel Los Piñades, captivated by the pure, elemental force that is people sharing sun-shine on a sandy beach. Then, turning suddenly to him, she simply asked:

– How could these people have torn themselves apart in such a bloody civil war? How?

There were tears in her eyes and for a moment he might have reached across the table and taken her hand. For a moment they could have looked like lovers to the waiter of the Hotel Los Piñades, leaning in the doorway, watching; but it passed quickly and instead they proceeded to talk about politics and ideologies and about how there was too much religion in the world; and that was that.

The week they were home, ETA started that summer's bombing campaign. Sara read about it in the paper: four small bombs exploded at popular seaside resorts in Cantabria, Northern Spain and there was an explosion outside a Barclays bank near Bilbao. The first Cantabria bomb exploded at about 12.15 pm local time on a seafront promenade in Laredo, damaging the walkway, breaking windows and sending a 25 metre pillar of smoke into the air. A second bomb went off about 40 minutes later next to the life-guard tower on the beach at Noja causing a loud blast but no damage.

It was short-lived, the thought of texting him. She considered the matter for a while and decided he would find out soon enough.

Hawks

"Hawks always make me happy and they were all out in the wild weather having a hard time making a living as the wind held the ground birds so close to cover."
– Ernest Hemingway in 'A Dangerous Summer'.

i

The Minister for the Environment glanced sideways to consider, a moment, the profile of his aide-de- camp. Young, with an Msc in Political Science and a Blackberry, she sat unbowed by their destination, speeding, as they were, towards the Border. It struck him as he looked away again, that she was childishly excited about what lay ahead of them.

The press office would be describing the venue for the release as: 'a remote location.' For the Minister, it remained: 'Bandit Country', and he shifted in his seat although there was no lack of room in the back of the four-by-four.

He had vetoed the use of a ministerial car; not because he feared attracting attention but because he knew the terrain they could expect.

— And make sure she's full before we leave the city, he had also insisted. I don't want us filling up with any dodgy diesel when we're there.

He could just imagine them getting stopped on the way back and dipped by customs and excise, intent on tackling fuel fraud, and the field-day the press would have. The politics of this new Executive, he had quickly learned, was full of such precautions.

In the course of the journey, Harry the driver regaled them with how he had driven professionally for twenty years, including stints in Washington and LA.

— Do you know how much one of those bullet proof Limousines weighs? He quizzed the rear view mirror.

— A tonne, the Minister unkindly responded.

— Correct, Harry confirmed. You don't want to brake suddenly in front of one of them.

— Were you always a chauffeur? The assistant asked.

— No. The height of the conflict, I drove one the bomb disposal transports. Now *that* thing weighs almost nine tonne.

— The equipment and all? The Minister suggested.

— Correct again, Harry replied. The 'robot' for instance. I was the only one could load that thing and disembark it without knocking any of its bits and pieces off and damaging the truck.

Approaching the outskirts of the last big town before the Border, the Minister ruefully watched the last raspberry rippling of a friendly flag flutter from a telegraph pole behind them; he noted too how his assistant really didn't register this; would she even, he wondered, notice the inevitable change in flag type and symbol.

Money from some previous administrations had bankrolled a new road system which looped them around the town in a by-pass and Harry pulled into the car-park of a golf-club, to the south, where a discreet police presence awaited them. The Minister lowered the automatic window to allow an officer to salute and, leaning in to keep his voice lowered, inform the Minister that they were not exactly sure where the location was.

— We don't have a regular rota of patrols in this neck of the woods yet; some community policing, that's all. Still relying a lot on the air, he explained, a little defensively.

The Minister knew that despite the official line, no-go areas still dotted the new post-process landscape.

— I could probably take you there myself, the Minister muttered. Only it would have to be in the dark.

The Minister had toured a duty there once only the landscape had been lunar and crepuscular to him then, viewed through the verdigris tinge of night vision glasses.

    — Anyway. The Minister raised his voice to bring Harry into the discussion. You've got it on sat-nav?

    — Correct!

    — You follow us, the Minister ordered the police officer.

The two vehicle convoy took off, heading into the hilly countryside. It looked knobbly and harsh to the Minister. Harry drove at a brisk pace but had to slow at intervals to allow the police Passat to catch up with them. After negotiating a number of country roads, and a few winding ascents, he indicated left and turned confidently up a rutted country lane at the summit of which they could see parked vehicles and a welcoming committee.

    — How do I look? He consulted his assistant.

    — Fix your fringe. There. Fine.

The minister got out, smile in place and hand extended towards the approaching dignitaries and officials. Two journalists, one from the local press, the other from the city, waited to one side; they both bore expensive looking cameras draped around their necks. The release, the Minister thought, would probably make the late edition.

There was to be little or no fuss or ceremony; after the initial welcome and exchanges, the Minister looked to the blue van and enquired:

— Well. Where are they?

The official from the bird trust gave a signal and a tall, attractive blond girl stepped lightly to the back of the van and extracted the cages containing the two birds of prey. She carried them to a clearing and aimed them out over the landscape.

— Minister, the official spoke, sweeping his hand in the direction of the cages. I proudly present our Red Kites.

The Minister stepped forward and recited his briefing, prepared by his assistant.

— It is a privilege to be part of this exciting re-introduction scheme. The Red Kite has been absent from this land for over two hundred years so it is particularly exciting to be officiating at the release of this pair of noble birds into what was once their natural habitat.

No mention of what had happened the previous year was made and the minister checked the two journalists for any tell-tale reaction, out of the practised corner of his eye.

— So. Without further ado, let us return them to this picturesque countryside and wish them well.

His assistant had scripted the word 'historic' to accompany 'picturesque', but the Minister omitted it. Surely, he thought to himself, there was a Heaney poem that could cover the likes of this.

Given the secrecy of the location, the audience was small, too small to warrant any significant applause; yet, the official from the bird trust was moved to put his hands together so that the two police officers, Harry and the journalists all felt the need to add some weight to the hand-clapping. Then the official stood aside and motioned the Minister in the direction of the cages whereupon his aide came forward and counselled:

– I think it more appropriate that you experts oversee the actual release into the wild.

– It would be a shame to miss a good photo-op, the journo from the city cautioned and he raised his eyebrows and the lengthy camera lens to press home the point.

– Very well, the Minister said. What do I do?

On instruction, the Minister approached the cages from behind, keeping his shadow from frighting the birds contained within. Bending, he lifted the two vertical grills simultaneously only to do a little jig backwards at the cannonade of wing, beaks and feathers exiting the cages. The photo-journalist from the city forgot all about the Minister, attempting, instead, to capture the two birds in flight, as they swooped out over the hills and pastures, only to lose them against the dark velour effect of a plantation of young, Scots pine on the slope opposite.

Behind him, the Minister brushed some plumage from his coat.

ii.

The Minister of Education spotted Doherty's mother in the audience; she was one of the group of school principals and other educational stakeholders from the local library board area gathered for the conference.

He had spotted her while running his eye over the attendees, trying to size them up to gauge which opening gambit to take. Then he made his decision.

— This, he announced, holding aloft a loosely bound sheaf of A4 pages. Is the script my advisors had prepared for me. However.

And here he looked around behind him, judged distances and tossed the presentation aside; it landed on and then proceeded to splay across the polished surface of one of the long conference tables supplied by the hotel, just stopping in time to droop Dali-like over the edge.

— I'm not going to bother yee with fancy words and phrases. Not when plain talking is what's needed. I'll dispense too with the power point; though you'd be impressed with the visual and sound effects.

The little laughter this raised allowed for a slight release of tension and for the Minister to glance at the
audience again. It also permitted Mrs Doherty, from
her view-point, to check out the reaction of the Minister's aides, standing discreetly to one side; neither of
them batted an eyelid. They had seen this theatre before. She knew his repertoire too, from having worked
on council and educational committees before the
Minister had graduated to the Executive; but she felt
the frisson effect it had on her less nuanced colleagues
around her.

   – While standards are high in many of our
schools, the Minister was continuing. There are still
too many children who struggle with reading, writing and using mathematics and too many young
people who leave school still lacking in skills and
confidence in these areas. What, he asked his audience. Are we doing about this tail of underachieve-
ment?

After the presentation and a short Q&A session, there
was a choice of coffee, tea, cold drinks and tray-bakes,
provided by the hotel. The Minister circled, all the
time homing in on the group where, cup and saucer in
hand, Mrs Doherty was holding forth.

   – Marie, he said at last, singling her out and shaking her hand. Marie and I go way back, he said by way
of explaining to the rest why he was about to spirit
her away.

— We were just talking about WALT, Minister, Mrs Doherty informed him. I take it you've made his acquaintance?

— Oh. I meet so many people it's hard to keep up, he replied. He was a little startled at the hilarity caused by his remark. But, if ladies and gentlemen you would excuse me: I want to steal Marie here away for a few moments.

— I must be getting that new build after all, she quipped, as he steered her aside by the elbow.

— I hear Doc- I mean Eamon's back home. Free-lancing or something.

— Yes. He was working for the Nationals. He's back in the city. Working on a book about the Middle East. Or is it Afghanistan? Why?

— Just enquiring after his health. I'd heard…

— I don't care what you've heard. She interrupted. He was on the 'phone just the other day. He assures me he's on the mend. So I take it I'm not due for a new school.

— You haven't applied for one, Marie.

— What do you want with him, Tom? He needs rest.

— Do you have a contact number for him? The Minister noted the look of concern on Mrs Doherty's face and added: I might have a story for him. That's all.

— Google him, then.

As she turned to re-join the group, the Minister had one last query for her.

— Who's Walt? He wanted to know.

iii.

WALT was an owl.

WALT was everywhere.

WALT was a new approach in schools.

WALT was what good teachers had probably been doing all along.

WALT was talking about learning more than teaching.

WALT was an acronym to remind the teacher to share ideas with children before or in the course of a lesson.

WALT was: We Are Learning To…

It was also driving one of Mrs Doherty's older teachers to distraction. For eight years Mrs Doherty had presided over a primary school that had transformed to integrated status through the amalgamation of a maintained and a controlled school, both with falling rolls. Felicity Orb had come along with the amalgamation. Mrs Orb had never been happy about the amalgamation; now, she was incredulous in face of the new teaching approaches.

— It's about active learning, Mrs Doherty had attempted to explain it, having summoned Mrs Orb to her office one day.

— Letting the children take over, Mrs Orb insisted.

– Not in the sense you mean, Mrs Doherty persevered. Giving them more opportunity to talk about their learning, yes. More group work. Less teacher talk.

– How will they learn if the teacher can't talk?

– No-one is saying the teacher can't talk. It's letting them talk too; talk about what they're learning. WALT: for example. She reminded Mrs Orb of the training they had been out to.

– That bloody bird again. Forgive my French. I should have gone before this.

Mrs Doherty had for some time been of the same view. She had already encouraged her governors to approach the employing authority about a 'package' for Mrs Orb. Otherwise, she warned them, she felt the woman was close to breaking point.

Hence the dread when she read the contents of the letter that arrived on her desk a week after her meeting the Minister. It was from the Health and Safety Executive, via the Department of Education re: 'Use of World War 2 Gas Masks in Schools'.

It began:

"As part of the Primary Curriculum, Key Stage 2, Strand 3 'Our World', pupils examine the reasons and effects of historical events, in particular The World Wars and The Great Famine.

During a recent visit to a school HSE Officers discovered a World War 2 gas mask being used in a display created by pupils in the school. The purpose of this memo is to make you aware of the attached information provided by the Imperial War Museum (IWM) in relation to the risks associated with these masks and guidance re their handling, display and storage."

Knowing that there were a couple of such displays in the school, Mrs Doherty shared the IWM information with her teachers that lunch-time, in the staff room. The problem was asbestos. It seemed that most British gas masks of WW2 had asbestos (blue and/or white) as a component of their filters. On top of this, the filters could also contain other respiratory irritants.

— 'Thus', she read aloud to her colleagues. 'No gas mask of WW2 vintage should ever be worn.'

She went on to explain how James, the caretaker, would dispose of each gas mask by placing it inside a plastic bag, sealing the bag and then repeating the process so that the object was securely 'double bagged'. Then they could be removed from the premises. One younger teacher suggested taking photos of the gas masks on the school digital camera before the removals; the images, she went on, could then be stored and uploaded and used in slide shows or reproduced for display purposes. The staff all agreed that this was a practical line of action to pursue.

    – As long as only James touches them. And that it's done and dusted today.

When she got back to her office, the secretary informed her that her son was on the 'phone.

    – It's me, Doc said, when he heard his mother pick up. How are you?

    – Oh. Just been decommissioning World War 2 gas masks, if you can believe it. It's a long story. How are you, more to the point?

    – I'm coming to visit, he replied. I've a bit of business to do. I'm arriving on the five train. Okay if I borrow the car for a day or two?

    – Of course. You might have to give me a lift into school though. I'll get something in for dinner for tonight. What sort of business?

    – Tell you when I see you. It's to do with birds of prey.

At this point, James burst into her office startling Mrs Doherty and ending the phone conversation.

    – It's Mrs Orb. You better see for yourself. She's locked herself in her room.

    – Good God, Mrs Doherty exclaimed when, hastening after James down the corridor, she got to Mrs Orb's classroom and looked through the vision panel in the door.

Wearing a variety of facial expressions ranging from concern to bemusement, the pupils sat, all eyes glued to the top of the classroom where Mrs Orb was in situ behind the teacher's desk, her head and face encased within her father's WW2 gas mask.

   – Unlock the door.

Only Mrs Orb's head moved when her Principal came into the classroom.

   – Good afternoon, children. I see Mrs Orb is demonstrating the use of a very vital piece of equipment that was designed to save lives during World War 2. I believe it belonged to Mrs Orb's father who, if I'm not mistaken, was decorated in that conflict. But, I'm afraid I must interrupt the lesson and ask you all to accompany Mr McAteer to the hall for a special assembly. We'll start with this row. Quietly now.

When the classroom was emptied, Mrs Doherty approached the desk.

   – Felicity, she said calmly. What are you thinking? You know the dangers.

However, she quickly realised that the woman's attention was distracted. Her eyes were both lost in and somehow enlarged by the eye-pieces in the mask and Mrs Doherty tracked the woman's rapt gaze to the cardboard owl, pinned to the display board. With his huge cartoon eyes, WALT seemed to mesmerise the woman in the mask.

iv

The Minister of Agriculture had raised the business of the birds of prey two days before Doc made the call to his mother.

The Minister met him at her constituency office; not the Assembly office perched high overlooking the City. Doc noted that there were still grills and security cameras masking the terrace house containing her party's headquarters; a thick set man showed him to the first floor office. She got up from behind her desk and came around to greet Doc, explaining how the Minister of Education had suggested him to her.

— You grew up together? She confirmed.

— We were from the same part of town, yes. I haven't seen him in years. Apart from the telly.

— Well: you've been away, I believe. Malachi, she delayed the man who had led Doc in. Be a dear and get us a cup of coffee. Mr Doherty?

— Coffee's fine; no milk. Call me 'Doc'.

— Sit here, she indicated one of two arm chairs sitting either side of a coffee table.

Doc noted a couple of political tracts on its surface along with some health and social services leaflets, in

Arabic and Cantonese, and, poking out from under the pile, a copy of 'Good Housekeeping'.

    — What's this all about, Doc asked as he sat down. I don't write propaganda. I'm a freelance.

    — Embedded with troops is freelance? She asked him in return.

    — I believe I managed to get my point of view across, he retorted.

    — Well. I don't think what I'm going to ask will compromise you too much, she assured him.

She leant forward and cleared a space on the table for Malachi to put down two mugs and a plate of custard creams. She handed Doc an old electioneering leaflet to use as a coaster for his mug.

    — Last year environmentalists released a pair of young Red Kites into the countryside, around the Border. All parties supported the re-introduction of what is an endangered species.

    — Bet the local farmers weren't too happy.

    — Within a month the bird wardens monitoring their progress found the remains of the two birds.

    — Shot or poisoned?

    — Shot.

    — Like I said: farmers.

    — Perhaps. Only: these birds weren't scatter-gunned out of the skies. They were 'picked out.' Removed.

– I don't follow.

– The forensics report indicated that each bird was brought down by a single shot; one neat bullet hole per bird. Wing tags and identifying leg rings were removed.

– Wait a minute. There's a forensics report for birds? Doc asked.

– They are a protected species. The police were called in.

– So, you're saying it wasn't a farmer's shotgun.

– It was a high velocity rifle. We're talking telescopic sights. The 'Real McCoy', the Minister assured him.

Doc sipped his coffee and considered this information. Then he looked at the Minister and said:

– In other words, the type of gun there isn't supposed to be out there anymore. Not after decommissioning.

– Add to the equation someone with the expertise to use such a gun; there's the potential for some mischief making from those more reluctant of our power-sharing colleagues; they could stall the peace process.

– But you said it happened last year. Surely they would have done something by now?

– That's right. We expected some reaction then. But strangely nothing's happened.

— So. What's the problem?

— Last week, a new pair of birds was introduced into the area. It got coverage in the papers. We want to make sure they don't meet a similar fate.

— You don't seriously think killing two birds, even an endangered species, will wreck the Process?

— Stranger things have happened. There's talks afoot to try and get those paramilitaries on the other side to disband. If our sharp shooter returns with the release of these birds: it could upset everything.

— So. You want me to protect these birds. How?

— You know the area. Have a look around for us. That's all. A day or two of your time. See if there is a real threat to the birds; if we should be worried.

— What if it turns out to be dissidents?

— Well, she paused for thought. That's okay. We can deal with that. As long as it's not one of our own. The 'conflict' is supposed to be over, after all.

Doc sat back to consider the offer. He looked the Minister in the eye.

— As a journalist, I can't be seen to be in your party's pay.

— You're doing it for the peace process, she cajoled him. And we'll only pay any expenses you accrue.

— In cash.

— Of course.

Doc got up and shook the Minister's hand.

— These birds, he said. They really are a protected species.

v

Freelander; Defender; Discovery; Warrior; Trojan.

Then there were Transit vans and Range Rovers and a few jalopies held together with baling wire and rust. These, the bird warden told Doc, were the sort of vehicles that had filled the car park of the local GAA Club that night. The hall had been crowded for the talk and slide show. The Bird Trust had organised with the Welsh Kite Trust for a farmer to come across and talk to the local people about the successful re-integration of the birds in Wales.

Doc's mother had put him in touch with the bird warden: she had visited Mrs Doherty's school a couple of times bringing with her Merlin, the Barn Owl and Percy, the Peregrin Falcon.

— Very Harry Potter, Doc had said to his mother.

— The children love it and Toni's an interesting girl. She's from Australia.

— Is she good looking?

Doc thought that she was as he sat opposite her now in her apartment.

— What sort of reception did your speaker get? He was asking her.

— Most listened to what he had to say. He assured them that he had lost no life-stock to any of the birds; that they were not a threat to human or animal.

— And how'd that go down?

— A lot of murmuring; a few more vocal dissenters; the 'usual suspects'. Some queried his credentials as a farmer. I had to intervene and tried to impress upon the audience that the birds did not prey on lambs or calves; that, in fact, they contributed to the environment by getting rid of vermin.

— When you say: the 'usual suspects' I take it you know some of these people.

— I've worked in this area for two years now. You get to know the locals. In particular the ones who react whenever you mention anything to do with conservation or the environment.

— Well perhaps you could give me some names. It might be interesting to talk to a few and get their angle on things. It would give a nice balance to my article.

They got up and went into the living room area where Toni had her computer set up; as she printed out a list of names for him she asked:

— Would you like a picture of a Red Kite? Do you even know what one looks like?

— Maybe we could arrange for you to take me out and show me the real thing.

— You'd need to apply officially, through the Trust.

As the printer clicked and shuddered, Doc looked around and spotted a fat paperback splayed open on the sofa.

— You don't strike me as a Grievous Angel, he said.

— What? She looked around at him.

— The book you're reading, he explained. It was a copy of David Meyer's 'Twenty Thousand Roads: The Ballad of Gram Parsons and his Cosmic American Music.'

— Oh. It's my boyfriend's; though I am enjoying it.

— Is he a bird warden too? Doc enquired.

— Part time. Summer he coaches surfing in Sligo or Donegal. He's there now. Rossnowlagh.

— I know it. I've swum there. You look like you surf yourself, he said.

— Used to, she admitted, handing him a list of names and some addresses. Don't do it much anymore.

— Why's that? Doc asked as he glanced at the print-out.

— Shark attack, she said.

— No way! He looked up at her.

— It's true. Look.

Toni raised her sweat shirt as far as her bra-line. A ragged Amazon of a scar ran along her rib-cage. Doc hesitated a moment and then he moved forward. Reaching out, he lightly traced the seam of raised tissue with his finger, looking up at her as he did so. She

returned his look and then lowered the garment, re-
moving his touch as she did so.

    – Do you have any scars, Mr Doherty? She asked
him on his way out.

    – None, Doc replied.

vi

Doc could feel the follower the minute he stepped
into the night-air. Resisting the urge to peer into the
shadows around him, he put his head down and went
in the direction of the public house he knew was located around the corner from Toni's flat.

    He made it there unscathed but was no sooner at
the counter, drawing the bar-maid's attention, than the
door he had just come through opened again admit-
ting a tall, athletic-looking man. Doc ordered a pint of
stout loud enough for the man who joined the counter a few stools down to overhear. Doc also enquired
aloud where the toilets were located, although he
knew well enough their whereabouts. He also knew
there was a second, side entrance to the bar on the
way to the toilet; this he used to make good his escape.
Outside in the side street, he broke into a run, heading
in the direction of the main street.

    Main streets no longer seem to mean much now
to town centres. This one had many blank and
boarded up shop-fronts and few people about; no-
one, at least, to witness a second figure emerging
from an entry and halting Doc in his tracks with

a punch to the solar plexus. The second man had caught up by this stage and both hauled Doc into the dark entrance.

— Careful now, one of them said with mock concern. You don't want to hurt yourself.

Doc slumped to the ground and immediately went foetal to protect his face and head. They kicked him anyway until the other one leaned down and said:

— This is just a little warning. There's worse to come if you keep sticking your nose where it doesn't belong.

With a parting kick, the pair walked off casually back up the side-street.

Doc lay a while groaning until he was suddenly alarmed anew at the approach of a third man. This one however, proceeded to help him to his feet, brushing him down with his hand as he did so.

— We can't send you back to your Ma in this state, he said.

— Who are you? Doc asked.

— Your minder, the youth replied.

— So. Why didn't you mind me?

— Are you joking? Those boys looked like they knew what they were doing.

Doc had to smile at the good sense his minder exhibited.

— Do you know who they were? Did you recognise them?

— Never saw them before, the youth replied. They're not locals.

Doc was leaning on the youth and seeing how well he could move; there didn't seem to be too much damage done and his face was unmarked so his mother would not suspect anything untoward had happened.

— No, Doc agreed. They're not locals. Can you help me to my car?

What he did not tell the youth about his two assailants was that both of them had English accents.

vii.

The age-old frontage of Tully's Saloon Bar was a feature of the small village square; the bar itself a hub of the countryside around. Inside, a group of old men sat watching the early afternoon racing. Doc spotted an assortment of daily newspapers, most folded to the back pages, though one, he saw, featured that day's notices and obituaries. At the counter, two back-packers looked out of place.

During Doc's most recent absence abroad, old man Tully had passed away; his son now stood behind the bar and Doc extended his hand:

— As I said on the phone: I'm sorry about your Da, he said. My mother wrote me about it.

   — You've time for a pint, Tully informed him glancing at the clock. They'll not be along for a while yet.

   — Who are your guests? Doc enquired, settling on a stool and nodding along the counter.

   — Danish, it seems. We're getting more and more tourists. It's not bad for business.

   — I've seen the sight-seeing tours in the city. Times have changed.

   — Not enough, Tully said, placing a pint of Guinness in front of Doc and dismissing payment.

Doc knew he was minder-less today. When he had told the youth where he was headed, the youth had politely declined to accompany him. Doc sat with his back to the street so it was Tully who saw the car pull up outside. There had been time for them to 'catch up', Tully having spent seven years travelling into Doc's town each day by bus to attend the same grammar school; seven years of regular disruption due to check-points and road blocks and bomb scares; just to get to school.

   — That looks like your appointment now.
Doc swivelled around and weighed up the situation: the driver was endeavouring to look past his own reflection in the pub window. Another youth craned around from the passenger seat also attempting to see into the premises.

   — Right. Best get it over with, he said. As he went to dismount from the bar-stool, he delayed a moment and looked quizzically at his erstwhile school companion.

– You did vouch for me? Didn't you?

– I told them who you were, Tully assured him. Even though I haven't seen you in years.

– I hope you didn't tell them that.

– Relax. They want you to do them a favour in return for the interview.

– Everybody wants me to be doing them favours, Doc said. Maybe I should invite Rosencrantz and Guildenstern along with me. They might even join up.

– There are more things, Horatio.... Tully said, then he wished him all the best.

viii.

Doc has been searched by experts. That time in Ramallah, for instance. Or South Ossetia, where they nearly stripped him looking for a reel of film. The youth that patted him down in the hallway of the farm-house was an airport amateur. In the parlour of the house, an older man sat patiently at the dining table and indicated the chair opposite to him when the youths brought Doc in. The man spent a while appraising Doc and Doc sat quietly and allowed him to do so. An Irish language paper, along with a parish bulletin, were the only things on the table between them. There was no talk of tea or coffee. The two youths moved around the table and took up positions just behind and to either side of the man. One leaned against a sideboard, the other folded his arms. Both eye-balled Doc.

   — Tully said something about you writing an article, the man announced suddenly.

   — That's right, Doc answered. Did he tell you what about?

   — Why don't you tell us?

Having spotted the paper, Doc began:

   — An iolar mhara.

The man remained impassive; the youths didn't budge.

   — I'm talking about the white-tailed sea eagle, Doc explained. 'An iolar mhara.' They were once our largest bird of prey, all around the coast of Ireland. Then they were driven to extinction. Well: now they're being reintroduced, and this is one of the areas designated for that purpose.

Doc paused to gauge how this piece of misinformation went down with his audience. A little internet research had revealed to Doc how the Golden Eagle Trust, in collaboration with the National Parks and Wildlife Service, were attempting to repopulate Co Kerry with the white-tailed sea eagle. No-one seemed moved to correct him; to tell him that locally it was Red Kites.

   — You haven't heard about this scheme, then? He asked them.

They all just looked at him. Doc decided to press ahead.

   — They tried to re-introduce the birds last year but someone shot them before they could settle and breed.

   — Farmers, the man suddenly said.

   — Maybe, Doc agreed. Except: it was done by an expert. We're talking high velocity rifle. One shot per bird.

   — So. What are you asking?

   — I suppose I was just wondering if 'he' was back.

Now there was some reaction. The two youths shifted slightly and looked at each other. The man sat back in his seat to better consider Doc's statement. The 'he' Doc referred to had been more than likely two or three individuals, drafted into the area at different times but whose reputation for deadly accuracy had coalesced into the single designation of 'the Sniper'; a title much dreaded by the Security Forces. Doc's allusion hovered between them for some time until, eventually, the man leaned forward again and said:

   — I don't know anything about any of that. But I can tell you we have our own experts; fully equipped and trained. We don't need 'him' any more.

   — And could one of your experts perhaps have shot the birds?

The three men stared at Doc and made him feel how derisory his query must have sounded to them.

— You may assure your readers, the man informed Doc. That this organisation is totally committed to all things 'green'.

They were still laughing at this statement when two vehicles pulled up and parked to the front of the house. One of the youths checked out the window and nodded to the man. He turned to Doc and asked him if he had a camera. Doc took this as some sort of accusation and protested:

— Sure you searched me in the hall there.

— I don't mean on you. In the car. We'd like you to record an important action.

— I've a digital one in the car, Doc confirmed, aware now of a bustle of activity outside, boots on gravel, car doors banging, orders in the air.
And shaking slightly as he got to his feet, he tasted it again: that heady mixture, the distinct, coppery tasting, cocktail of fear and excitement. Adrenalin.

He almost smacked his lips.

ix.
The six men were all in masks now; and armed.

They had driven some five miles from the farmhouse, Doc following in his mother's car. They all parked beside a derelict barn and, unloading their garb and equipment, proceeded to trek across some fields before coming down onto a wide country road. Some of the number went into kneeling mode in the hedge-row. Two waited in the middle of the road. Doc quickly realised it was a check-point; not an ambush.

He could identify the man by his eyes, enlarged as they were by the ski-clava which he wore. Raising his camera enquiringly, Doc received an affirmative nod and began to take pictures. They heard the rattle of a trailer and all watched as a car and horsebox appeared around the bend behind them. The two men waved the vehicle to a stop and while one of them quizzed the driver about identity and destination, the other stood on tip toes and looked into the horse box. There was a horse inside, he announced. The next vehicle was a builders' van; it got a desultory search and drove on. Those drivers that had them, produced licenses. A mother with children showed such anxiety that they quickly waved her on. Another motorist cheerfully addressed one of the masked men by name. Then there was a long interval of inactivity.

– Fuck, one of the men in the road said when the police car appeared.

It just cruised casually around the bend, coming from the direction of the town and came to a sudden halt at the sight of the check-point. Doc had been facing the other way but turned at the sound of the brakes. It was an unmarked Passat, but the two occupants were obviously in uniform and he snapped their round faces as they peered down the road at them. He could make out that the driver was female.

Quickly, he turned his lens on the masked men to see what they would do. Although all the guns were trained on the police car, most heads were angled slightly in the direction of the man in his ski mask. He stood frozen to the spot. Everyone waited.

– Nobody fire, he eventually ordered and Doc began to wonder if the guns were loaded or if the youths were sufficiently trained to engage the enemy.

Instead, they all watched as the policeman in the passenger seat counselled his colleague and slowly the car performed a three point turn and in unexcitable fashion drove back the way it had come, back around the bend.

When he looked again, the check point had been disbanded, the participants climbing into the fields and heading back to the barn. By the time Doc got there, they were gone.

He had trouble with his trembling fingers, extracting the memory card from his digital camera. When he managed to pinch it out, he hid it away in the glove compartment and stood a moment leaning on the car. He realised he was listening for the helicopter. Then he wondered if there were any left in the country; if they hadn't all been dispatched to Afghanistan. The sudden swoop of the bird startled him but he managed not to alarm it as it alighted on the exposed rafter of the barn. Though only a young bird it appeared huge to him; at rest, yet its eyes sharp, alert; its head slowly rotating to take in the land around it. Afraid to move, Doc stood, his empty camera useless in his hands, staring at the bird. Then they both heard the far-off racket of rotor-blades and leaning forward it seemed to fall into its huge wing-span only to rise suddenly and disappear off over the fields.

x.

Back in the village square, Doc rang Toni. He described the bird and she confirmed his sighting for him.

— You're privileged, she told him. I hope you got a picture.

— Why don't I meet you for a drink tonight and I can show you, he suggested.

— Sorry. I can't, she replied.

— Is your boyfriend back? He asked.

— No. It's not that.

— Why not then? He pressed her on the point.

— The same reason I don't go into the water much anymore, she told him.

After she had hung up, Doc sat for a while, mulling over what she had said. Then he shrugged it off and unfolded the list of names she had supplied him with the previous day.

Fifteen minutes before punching the farmer in the face, Doc had watched the woman of the house load camogie sticks, sports bags and two children into the family saloon and drive down the lane past where he was parked. Doc then went on up to the house and when he

mentioned an article about the birds, the farmer agreed
to a brief interview. Doc didn't let on that the farmer's
name had been top of the list. For the most part the
farmer fielded and evaded Doc's questions.

 — I don't care what the conservationists say,
he said at last. These are hard times for farmers.
We can't afford to run the risk of losing life-stock.
Or racing pigeons; do you know how much one of
them costs?

 — But the point is: these birds aren't really birds of
prey; they're more carrion birds, Doc explained.

This statement seemed to get the farmer's attention;
but, he still said:

 — You're wasting your time. I can't help you.

At this, Doc sighed and sat back; he looked around
him; he took in children's school books, the local paper and a magazine. As the farmer made to get to his
feet by way of bringing the talk to a close, Doc did
a double take. This was because the magazine was
a title he had seen numerous times, only in Quon-
set huts and mess halls, in sandbagged departure
lounges, discarded on aircraft seats, left in latrines;
but it came as a shock to see it now. So he got up and
landed his punch. The farmer sat back down in his
seat and stared.

 — I thought you said you were a reporter, he
said.

— A war one, Doc explained and, pointing at the copy of 'Soldier of Fortune', he asked: Now, who shot the fucking birds?

Rubbing the side of his face, the farmer had a question for Doc.

— Have you ever, he asked, heard of 'Blackwater'?

And this time it was Doc's turn to sit back down in his seat.

xi.

— A Brit! The Minister of Agriculture exclaimed.

— Well, a mercenary. We don't know what nationality. The farmers never actually met him; they got him off the internet.

Doc had just explained how a collective of farmers, concerned for their livestock, had paid for the shooter.

— No. It was a Brit alright, she insisted. It explains why no-body kicked up any fuss at the forensics last year. They've known all along who did the shooting: one of their own.

— Well. An ex-one of their own.

— And it explains a conversation my assistant had with the Minister for the Environment's aide: seems that if any more of the birds get shot –

— Let me guess: it'll be by shot-gun, Doc interrupted.

— That'll be the official line, she conceded.

– They don't want the 'House of Beer Mats' up here on the hill collapsing any more than you.

– A cynical way to put it, but it does seem that it'll take more than shooting listed wild-life to stop the process. Still, we also agreed to do our utmost for the birds.

– Doves defending hawks, Doc said.

– Hey, she warned. That sounds like a headline. You know you can't write about any of this.

By this stage, Doc was stuffing his envelop of expenses into his jacket pocket.

– Don't worry, he assured the Minister. No-body wants to read about here anymore.

– So. What next for you? She asked him.

– I hear there's trouble in Honduras, he replied. The next time, however, was not a shot-gun. Alphachloralose killed the bird. It was found dead beside a rabbit that had been laced with the illegal poison.

– Red kites are scavengers as opposed to predators and therefore pose no threat to small agricultural animals or pigeons. It is totally irrational to poison these birds which are a wonderful addition to our environment, the Minister for the Environment said.

His mother had enclosed the newspaper report in one of her letters. He read it by the light of a blood-red sunset in the desert. Then, when he heard the whine behind him, he reached up, pulled his goggles on and stood up to watch the sand drama that always happened here every time a helicopter lifted into the sky or when one came back in to land again.

C-PAP

The old man hated a bad night's sleep for dreams were the only stories anyone ever told him now.

— Don't I tell you things? Maggie had protested.

— Sure when do I ever see you? He rebuked, but in a softer, more playful tone. You've obviously found something more interesting to occupy you.

— I'll visit you when you get your hip done, she insisted.

Now he was locked in the relentless sleep of a coma; and Maggie wondered if dreams could struggle through to him there. During the routine hip operation, he had aspirated and his lungs had filled with fluid. He was immediately transferred down the motorway to the ICU in Craigavon. They shaved off his great white beard and attached him to a ventilator with the C-pap mask clamped to his face. The machine made a sucking, slavering sound and Maggie said:

— You sound like Darth Vader.

— Who? A sharp voice made her start. She looked up and saw the old man's elderly sisters standing at the door.

– I was just saying the mask makes him look like Douglas Bader.

– Who are you talking to? Violet asked, coming in and looking around the hospital room.

– Him of course. The nurse says to talk to him.

The two sisters stared at Maggie for a long instance before each bending over the old man and kissing his forehead. The Filipino nurse followed them in and Maggie sought her support:

– Isn't that right, nurse? Aren't we supposed to talk to him?

– Talking is important, the nurse concurred. She checked the readings on the monitor and spoke to the old man: And how are we today, Frank?

– He was christened Francis, Violet interjected.

– Good, the nurse said to her though she glanced at Maggie. It is important you tell us this: little things like that might help us reach him. How are you today, Francis?

– I've got to run, Maggie said, picking up her coat. I'll ring you tonight, she said to the two sisters. Then, from over by the door, she called to him:

– I'll see you tomorrow. Frank.

Then there was only the flat motorway-land back to the city. There was a barn, emblazoned with words from the Old Testament. There was a sign to a bird sanctuary and discovery centre. There was a curious herd of Cherry-pickers craning hydraulic necks over the security boundary of Higher Access Ltd; and there was the derelict remains of the Maze prison across the fields. Security towers still stood, skeletal and erect, spaced equidistantly along the outer wall, rust wounds visible from the road. A Sports Minister had recently announced plans to transform the 360 acre site, recommendations for which included a sports zone; an international centre for conflict transformation; a rural excellence and equestrian zone; a village of office, hotel, entertainment and leisure facilities; a light industry zone; a community zone; an area for arts and iconic artwork; landscaping/parkland and transport infrastructure. 'It doesn't have to be a dream,' he had said on the news.

— The 'jury', the Consultant had told her before she had left the hospital. Is still out, as regards his chances of recovery. But we must have faith.

Given the old man's illness, Maggie took the few days' leave she had been carrying over. She worked with young children, as a speech therapist, based in one of the poorest wards in the city yet, despite her efforts to get through to parents, the rate of non-attendance at appointed times was very high.

She rang ICU, early the next morning. She recognised the accent and said,

— Is that you Cristina? She had read the nurse's name on her badge.

— Yes. How are you? There has been no change. But he has had a good night.

When she hung up, Maggie decided to take her daily run early and then go to the hospital.

Her outdoor run-route wound through the woods in Belvoir Forest Park. She limbered up in the car-park and then went off down the wide rutted path into the woodland. The forest produced a fox for her that morning, cutting furtively across her in the mist. The sun came out and illuminated great napalm bursts of autumn in the trees. The sights and sounds and the exertion set her heart beating faster and she increased her speed.

However, it had also rained the night before and the forest smelt 'off', like dishcloths left to lie too long. The river level was up and there were clumps of beer froth rotating swiftly on the current. She kept her head down then and concentrated on her breathing. Her circuit took her, eventually, back to the car park but with a punishing incline to attack before reaching it. She forced a fast finishing pace on herself and, lungs bursting, her momentum carried her exultantly onto the level tar macadam surface where her car sat, facing the view out over the valley. Leaning over the bonnet of the car, she fought to get her breath back and said impulsively:

— Thanks be to God.

She straightened up with a shocked expression on her face and looked around her. She looked up at the sky. She looked out across the valley. She felt ambushed by this overpowering sense of thankfulness that invested the phrase she had just uttered with something other than rote or reflex. A single magpie flew like a torn piece of newsprint off over the well preserved mound of the forest park's motte and bailey; an airplane climbed above her out of the Harbour Airport, the company logo legible on the fuselage, and above it another bird wheeled and circled, this one too far up to distinguish.

— Jak sie masz? She enquired of the old man. That means: 'How are you doing?' she explained. Remember: I told you I was learning Polish.

She had not, however, told him about the engineer from Gdansk.

— His name's Marek, she told the old man. You'd like him. He's earning five times here what he can at home. When he gets back, I'll bring him to visit you.

She looked at the old man's frozen features. He had grown gaunt, cadaverous; through the opaque mask she saw how the intubation was deforming his mouth. She searched about for another phrase and said:
— Kockam cie. This time, she did not translate.

Cristina came in and saw the old man's fingers flinch.

— Look! She exclaimed. There is a reaction. He must recognise what you are telling him, she declared.

In their excitement, they reached across the old man in the bed and clasped each other's hands.

The forest park was asmoke with frozen fog. A musketry of mist billowed off the meadow in the middle, as if she had stumbled upon some recently vacated furious battlefield. The forest seemed held in place by frost, shrubs and bushes clamped by ice and going nowhere; yet through it all, her long legs confidently carried her, her lungs aglow with the frozen air. Today, she felt empowered to extend her run. She ran along the towpath as far as Shaw's Bridge, named for one of Cromwell's generals. He had built a bridge there to trundle canon across the Lagan and so lay siege to the city. Now motor traffic roared past for the city had long since encircled and subsumed the site and Maggie was glad to cross over and turn back once more into the rural illusion of the woodland.

When she got home there was still no message on her answering machine. The dictionary sat beside the phone.

Three days later, Maggie risked camera-vans and speed traps to get to Craigavon: Cristina had rung to say that Frank had regained consciousness.

— Maggie, the old man 'Don-Corleoned' when she appeared around the door.

The mask had been removed.

— Stop talking, Violet commanded; then, to Maggie: The nurse says his throat's been rubbed raw by that old tube.

— Welcome back, Maggie greeted him.

— It's thanks to all our prayers and novenas, Winnie declared. Our knees are near wore to the bone.

— And we're out a fortune lighting candles, Violet added.

The old man looked at Maggie and rolled his eyes. She squeezed his hand and smiled.

— Let's not forget the part played by the hospital staff, she asserted.

— If you ask me, they're the ones put him here in the first place.

On the way out she stopped the ward sister.

— C-pap, she said. What does it stand for?

— Continuous. Positive. Airflow. Pressure. The woman replied.

— It certainly does, Maggie agreed.

By the time she got to drive the old man home, banners had begun to appear tethered to bridges and fly-overs. They enjoined people to: 'Say No To The Maze.' The old man looked quizzically at her and she told him about the recent announcement from the Sports Minister.

— Seems the IRFU and GAA and IFA have consulted. There's a hard-core opposition nonetheless.

He thought a moment and, with his voice not fully recovered, wrote a reply on his note-pad. He held it up for her to see and taking her eyes off the road briefly she read: 'Don't say No to the Maze. Say No to the Minotaur.'

   — What are you on about? she said. It's well saying you're back in the land of the living.

Maggie had to haggle with the two aunts but eventually obtained money enough to allow her to write a respectable cheque, payable to the ICU Social Committee. This she delivered a week later.

   She rang the bell located in the waiting room, and waited. There was standing room only and everyone else there looked drawn and worried. The TV was on but with the mute symbol visible on the screen and few paying any attention to the silent news item being broadcast. Eventually the ward nurse appeared and, recognising Maggie, she beckoned her into the ward. Presenting the cheque, Maggie was surprised by the woman's muted response.

   — We really do mean thank you, Maggie felt it necessary to press home the point. We thought we'd lost him.

   — Forgive me, the nurse said, realising Maggie's confusion. It's just we've had some bad news. Remember Cristina?

   — Of course. Uncle Frank's favourite.

— That mud-slide, the nurse explained. It was her village. She hasn't been able to make contact with her family. It's just terrible.

Stunned, Maggie stood and realised what the flickering images of devastation on the waiting-room TV had been trying to report.

Maggie ran past the trees. She ran hard on the iron-hard, frozen mud. She ran pell-mell; at full tilt. She held nothing in reserve for the many inclines and obstacles that lay in her way. She ran until she could run no longer and then ran some more. She skidded on a patch of black ice and kept her balance and ran on. She pulled up and doubled over, hands clamped vice-like on each thigh. She heaved and spat and ran again, alarming a Labrador that had been lolloping playfully up to her. The dog's owner stepped out of her way. She ran every ounce of energy out of her until, stumblingly, she somehow regained the empty car park.

She realised it had begun to snow. Snow had been forecast all over Europe; now, here it was, sweeping in obliquely from the east. Great rinds of snow were uncurling from a heavy evening sky, dropping into the dark, numinous forest below. A soft sieving of snow was settling on the Christmas pudding shaped surface of the motte and bailey. Trembling, she straightened up and looked long and hard at this great mound of earth.

Then, without a word, she turned away, got into her car and drove off. The angry, speeding arc her tyres made was quickly covered over by the snow.

Meanwhile in Mindanao, the Moro Islamic Liberation Front (MILF) had called a temporary ceasefire to allow emergency aid to reach the stricken villages located there. In a historic break with the past, Benigno Aquino, the Philippines president, announced his willingness to meet with rebel leaders to seek a longer lasting peace.

"The road map on the table is real," said Teresita Quintos Deles, the presidential adviser on the peace process.

On a visit to Dublin, Jun Mantawil, head of the MILF secretariat and a member of the front's negotiating team told journalists: "Northern Ireland is a very similar situation to us."

"The Good Friday Agreement is a model for us, he said. "It is very encouraging."

Squirrels

People's dogs seemed to snap a lot that credit crunch Christmas; and snarl. There was increased strum and tension to leashes and leads. Handlers' calls and curt commands barely tamed aggression; even the normally more mild mannered, micro-chipped, middle class canines. Some owners seemed past caring: the lady that late afternoon, for instance, remaining in her car while her two poodles growled round Gregory doing his warm-up routine. Gregory had, for some weeks now, started to keep his track suit bottoms on, as protection for his bare legs.

The forest park itself seemed the worse for wear, what with lay-offs and downsizing among the Forest Service staff. The tow path along the disused canal, and the forest floor, were strewn with dog-crunch log debris. The riverbank was be-whiskered with litter; goatees of plastic bags drooped from shrubs and branches; there were Loch Ness humps of car tyres in the water. Dog foul and cigarette butts were back. These muffled the crisp, cereal crunch of autumn underfoot which he had enjoyed in previous years' running. Beer cans lay crushed and gutted on stony shoals where the locals had begun to fish the river for Brown trout, Rainbow trout, Perch, Pike, Rudd or Eels.

Gregory was convinced the residents had lost their patience with the traffic of joggers and dog lovers who drove through their housing estate to access the forest park and had begun to 'play chicken' with them, asserting right of way with vans and four-by-fours, refusing to yield even when any obstruction was on their side of the road. There seemed little goodwill that Christmas though many of the houses persevered with outdoor decorations; house fronts fretful with winking fairy lights; plastic lit-up figures giving vague, ambiguous gestures as Gregory drove past on the way to the forest car park.

– Euripides pants, you pay for them, he warned the two persistent poodles, at which their ears spiked up and they backed off, yapping at him.

He decided to abandon his warm-up and jogged out of the car park and down the steep gradient towards the forest. Over his shoulder he saw the woman sit on heedless in her car.

At the moment, Euripides was very much on his mind. His commission to write an update of 'The Bacchae' and stage a production of it had fallen foul of the recession. It was why he was late going for his run. His mobile had run down so he had used the crackling, land line to lodge his protest at the Arts Council's decision to withdraw his funding.

He reminded the Arts Officer how Pina Bausch's Tanztheater company had successfully choreographed Christophe Gluck's opera *Iphigenie auf Tauris*, a few years ago. He pointed out how the ratings and box office takings had both been high.

— The Council just doesn't see the play's relevance at the moment, she explained. There's no stomach for deus ex machina, these days.

— Then you haven't read my treatment. Of course it's relevant, he insisted.

— What? A bunch of mad women tearing — what's his name — to pieces.

— Pentheus. His name's Pentheus. And you obviously haven't seen the pictures of the child benefit riots last week.

— Clutching at straws, my dear. No. Euripides is on hold. Sorry.

Replacing the phone in the cradle, Gregory had looked out at the darkening afternoon and considered putting off his run. He recalled how the critic W. G. Arnott had argued that Euripides deglamorized violence, describing the revenge narratives of the plays as 'gangland killings'. He recalled how popular the play had been in antiquity and that it had been a favourite of the emperor Nero. With his mind awhirl with such deliberations, Gregory decided it would make better sense to run off his dismay and frustration.

Just down the hill from the car park was Corbey Wood. Entering it, everything seemed suddenly to darken in tone and Gregory was just making his mind up to do the shorter of his customary run routes when the terrier attacked.

In the gloom he saw it coming. Jaws snipped at Gregory's calf muscles and the dog's manic movements almost tripped him up. Gregory drew up and hissed at the dog in an effort to repel him but as the terrier came at him again, Gregory sank the toe of his running shoe into its soft underbelly and it flew off into a clump of bushes and remained there.

Then, in the sudden silence that ensued, Gregory heard the others.

There was a baying from the far side of the river and he heard loud splashes as of heavy weights dropping into the water. A few water fowl scattered panic stricken into the darkening sky; a couple teetered past him on Ray Harryhausen stop motion spindly legs. Then Gregory had the impression of dark forms coming like bullets through the undergrowth. It was at least two dogs, both larger than the terrier to judge by the commotion coming his way.

So Gregory ran. He ran through a zigzag of tree trunks. He ran in the direction of the car park. He ran until the worn soles of his trainers skated on a rink of loam and compacted leaf mould. Keeping himself upright, he gained better purchase on a floor of pine needles and this surface empowered a full on sprint towards the incline to the car park. He ran and his fists went like pistons; his heart hammered. But at his back he could clearly hear the two dogs drawing near. He could hear the jingle-bell of broken chain link and buckles and identity tags. He could hear the growing growling. Then, almost at the edge of the wood, not having warmed up sufficiently, his hamstring snapped and he cried aloud. Forced to pull up, Gregory turned at bay against the trunk of a big cypress.

The story goes that around 406 BC, Euripides left Athens at the invitation of King Archelaus 1 of Macedonia to stay in the city of Pela. It was here he lost his life. One day, out walking in the grounds of the royal estate, the playwright was attacked and killed by the King's hunting dogs.

Gregory was thinking about a stick or broken branch with which to ward off his attackers; he was thinking about throwing rocks – car keys? – when he spied the two dogs in the half- dark, teeth bared and tearing towards him, surging out of the gloom. Then one of them was shot.

There was a flash first of all – it lit up the high visibility, reflector zip-lines and piping on his jogging top – then the deafening report of the gun. When he saw, moments later, that it was a hand-gun, he could not believe the roar it had made. The stench of cordite hung in the air, like the aftermath of a firework.

All Gregory could do was stare as, yelping now, the wounded dog took off the way it had come, overtaken and outstripped in no time and abandoned by its companion.

Numb, Gregory turned and watched as a slight figure appeared dwarfed by the outsized hooded parka it wore. The hand that held the gun was still extended.

   – I think you got one of them, Gregory managed to mumble, unable to avert his eyes from the fire-arm.

   – Fuckers frighten the squirrels, a woman's voice replied. So do joggers.

And, as she continued to walk past him, Gregory saw them. Pinioned through their sinewy hind legs, with string or wire, as an angler would a catch of fish, a dead stole of grey squirrels was draped over the woman's shoulder. Their little pins of teeth seemed to phosphoresce in the gloom; *Sciurus carolinensis* or American Grey, as opposed to the red or *Sciurus vulgaris*, deemed indigenous due to being found among Irish mammals listed in Latin by an Irish monk, Augustin, in the 17th century.

   – Car park's up that way. You should go.

She snapped on a torch-light and going down on her hunkers, examined the forest floor. She checked her gun, clicked the safety and shoved the gun into the pocket of the parka jacket, thus freeing her right hand to rake the pine needles and mulch with her fingers.

  — Blood, she declared, regarding her finger tips in the beam; but she seemed really to be addressing herself.

Gregory remained silent. Then she extinguished the light and darkness washed in all around them. When his eyes adjusted he could just make out her fading form; going off the way the dogs had gone.

For a brief moment he considered calling after her; however, her austere demeanour did not seem to invite or require any expression of gratitude or thanks on his part.

    Instead Gregory hobbled painfully back to the car. Up out of the wood, there was a modicum of light in the car park. An infrequent business flight roared overhead, out of the alcoholic airport; he looked up at the flashing lights on the wing-tips. The aeroplane seemed suddenly so distant, so out of reach.

    The car park was empty except for his own car and the small Renault belonging to the poodle woman. He thought of their interference leading to his aborted warm-up and the pulled hamstring. Looking around he could see no sign of them. This prompted him to peer more closely in the direction of the car itself. He thought he could make out the form of the woman still upright in the driver's seat. He considered limping over to her and warning her about staying too late in such a location. However, something about the stillness of the car, the immobility of the woman as she sat facing the darkening valley where the other woman hunted, gave him pause for thought.

Instead he clumsily unzipped a pocket to retrieve his car keys. He banged his head and barked his shin getting into the car. There was much pain trying to fold his injured leg in under the steering column. When he turned the key in the ignition, the baleful orange moon appeared on the dashboard reminding him he had been running on empty. Checking first, through side windows and rear windows and windscreen, he forced himself back out again and placing his hands on the bonnet, he bounced the vehicle up and down. The mixture of slosh and vapour in the tank would, he hoped, be enough to get him away from the forest. He could sense it retracting in on itself, all around him, reverting to some dark and timeless and primordial form. Looking a last time at the woman's car he got himself back into his own.

When he switched the engine on, he gaped as his head-lights lamped a constellation of steely eyeballs, studded green and rivet-like in the undergrowth across from him. Gunning the engine then, Gregory roared out of the forest car park and sped through the housing estate and raced along the ring-road, all the time worrying as he went in case there was not enough fuel in the tank to get him home.

The Man with the Banana Joke

Frank had been searching for a green hand with no mottles on the surface of the skin. If he got the timing right the fruit would ripen slowly and there'd be no risk of the children turning their noses up at the prospect of bringing the bananas to school as part of a packed lunch the following week. It was in the middle of this rummage that the old man, tartan flat cap and rain coat, approached him and told him the banana joke.

Frank always shopped on the same day; a week later, he spied the same old man relating the same joke, on this occasion to an attractive house-wife. He was some distance from them, over by the broccoli, rocket and sprouts, and so out of earshot, but he could tell it was the same joke when the old man started to pound his scrawny chest, aping King Kong. Frank recognised this punch line.

The house-wife laughed politely and pushed her shopping trolley on down the ready-made meals aisle.

A few weeks later the old man was there again, doing his shopping but also, when in the vicinity of the bananas, alert to the possibility of entertaining another customer with his routine. Unlike the large trolley that Frank used, the old man needed only a basket, which he pushed around in the smaller trolley frame designed for those customers with fewer articles to purchase.

From that first early autumn night, right up as far as Christmas, Frank omitted to mention the old man and the joke to his wife and children. It was as if, once away from the neon-lit, fluorescent precincts of the supermarket, the old man slipped from his memory; even though the children were of an age to have enjoyed the joke. He did recount it once though, one Friday, during early evening, after work drinks in The Garrick Bar, at the corner of Chichester Street and Montgomery Street; however, the spectacle he conjured up of the old man with his skinny fists and their liver spots provoked the greater laughter from his colleagues.

The supermarket had a policy of hiring senior citizens alongside recent school leavers and students employed part-time. The older ladies on the cash registers got to trust Frank with his shopping routine and, piecing together snippets of weekly chat and banter, they began to build up their profile of a hard-working, respectable husband – to judge from certain tell-tale items purchased – and father, what with Coco-pops and fruit shoots, twelve packs of Tayto and Penguin biscuits, sometimes Snickers; Frubes and Frosted Shreddies. The lady in the off-license part of the supermarket could note his change from old world to new world wines and, then, an interest in rosé. They would know where he intended to go for holidays and tell him, in turn, their own destinations. Price rises, credit crunch, poor parking facilities, exchange rates were topics that frequently arose as the items nudged one another along the conveyor-belt counter and Frank packed systematically: fridge and freezer stuff all organised; detergents, firelighters and washing up liquids in the same bag so as not to 'tack' foodstuffs, toiletries together; all aimed at making the unpacking easier and orderly in the house. Watching this, every-so-often one of them would comment:

— She has you well trained.

— You can say that again, Frank would say.

Although 'she' had accompanied him on a few occasions, mostly during commercial holiday times, the weekly shop was one of his allotted chores and the staff never really registered her. In the beginning he would tell her about the various chats he had had but, as the topics and subject matter never really changed that much, he told her less and less. Occasionally she would enquire after his 'friends' but eventually this faded too.

Supermarket shopping was nothing new to him. At university, he and his flatmates would have taken it turn about to do a weekly shop with their collective kitty money. It became a regular fantasy for them to see if they could spot a bored young house-wife, leaning over, sifting through the frozen produce, requiring help to reach something from off a high shelf. Such encounters, however, never occurred; there were girls their own age anyway, and everyone, sooner or later, seemed to get married. Now, much older, he found himself looking again.

At first, it was not a deliberate scrutiny; it was more a matter of peripheral vision, suddenly spotting someone, noticing a pretty face. It added some excitement to the prospect of doing a shop. Then, he was suddenly alarmed to find himself looking at women's breasts. He had always enjoyed these but had never ogled them as he now feared he was doing. His fear was terrifyingly realised when a female colleague one day at work startled him by saying:

— Well? What do you think?

— What do I think? He had stammered, looking askance at her.

— I'd be interested in your opinion, she coolly persisted with her line of questioning. Your evaluation.

— They're gorgeous, he at last assented.

There was an awful pause and then she said:

— Right answer.

The dalliance did not last long but it caused consternation and alarm among the ladies at the tills. First, the regularity of the Thursday night shop became disrupted. Then, and they knew this sign well, the list of items grew less and less and they looked sadly and knowingly at one another. This diminution of contents had nothing to do with the economic down-turn and recession. The last time Frank visited the store, he only needed a basket-full and he avoided his old 'friends' by qualifying for and passing through the 'ten items or less' Express Till.

    – Do you have a reward card, sir? The young girl there asked him.

    – Not on me, he apologised. I'm sorry.

He did once try to tell her about the banana joke and about the old man and his accosting customers. However, there was something needing done, some more pressing issue, and it interrupted his account and he never returned to it. Indeed, he must have stopped noticing the old man at all and he could not remember even when the old man stopped making his appearance. By that stage, it seems, he had begun to notice other things.

A year later, he saw his wife with another man in the mezzanine bar at the Opera. It was the interval and the people he was with were discussing the merits of the first half of the performance when he spied her through the throng. And she took his breath away.

She was talking intently with her tall companion. He vaguely recognised him as someone who was in the media. When she saw him approach she froze. Taken aback by this reaction he too stopped in his tracks, suddenly uncertain and the companion looked up and then, with due pause, leant down to her, whispered in her ear and withdrew a few feet.

Frank advanced and, stopping, declared simply:

— You look beautiful.

She moved towards him suddenly and he instinctively inclined forward as if to be kissed. Instead, he felt her tiny, little fists punch him furiously on the chest; an awful strangulated sound issued from her throat. He straightened up but made no other attempt to defend himself. Opera House people around them stopped and stared as he stood and took this pummelling. Then the announcer announced that the drama was about to restart, and the bell rang, and the tall companion re-appeared to take Frank's wife gently by the arms and lead her away; back into the auditorium.

Left standing there alone, Frank suddenly remembered the banana joke; and, for a moment he almost thought it funny. He almost, for a moment, laughed out loud.

The Girl with the Greek Haircut

Carmel watched her friend swimming in the villa's pool. She had come out onto the small balcony of her bed-room and was gazing down. With the heat of the Cretan sun, Carmel knew not to press on the wrought iron railing that wound around her.

— Come on down and cool off, Aine was shouting up to her now.

The measured splashes from the pool had just woken her from her afternoon nap; factor in the heat and the incessant skirling sound of the cicadas in the trees, and she was not surprised to feel a little light-headed. Then, when she looked down again, she was suddenly dazzled by the sight of the sun catching on the ruffled water of the pool and Aine in the middle moving meshes of golden water around her in a dreamy semaphore of slow-motioned, undulating arms and legs.

— Coming, Carmel called back.

The one piece bathing suit she preferred to the bi-kini she had brought as back-up was already dry despite that morning's dip in the pool. She swiftly fitted into the costume, made a face at the mirror and, lifting a Larsen, she flip-flopped down to the pool-side. A tall wall preserved their privacy. From the balcony you could see part of the property opposite and then toasted shrub-land and stunted olive trees leading off to where the main road declared itself in sporadic gusts of dust clouds.

From the pool-side, Aine's motion in the water appeared less measured: she held her head determinedly out of the water not wanting to get her hair wet. They had rowed when unpacking and Carmel realised she had forgotten to pack a hair-dryer; everything had been so last-minute, deciding to suddenly book the break the way they had. It meant they had to share Aine's dryer and straighteners which was a nuisance needing them at the same time. There was a dryer in the villa but it was as weak and asthmatic as the air-conditioning. They rowed over the air-conditioning too. A notice from the owner warned residents not to tamper with the dial; Aine had ignored this and turned the dial up.

– You've got to keep your windows closed for it to work correctly, Aine had argued.

Sometimes, one or other of them would wake up in the middle of the night shivering. Most times, they found the heat in the house oppressive.

With neck erect and her red hair bunned-up out of the water, Aine swam to where Carmel stood.

   – I looked in on you earlier but you were out for the count.

   – I'm exhausted, Carmel conceded with a laugh. Doing nothing.

   – Isn't that why we're here, Aine replied before pushing herself off the side into the deep end again.

Aine had claimed that they were here so that Carmel could get a well earned rest: why she was angry that first evening when she had caught Carmel accessing work emails on the Blackberry she had smuggled into the villa.

Sighing to herself, Carmel stepped down into the warm water of the pool; submerging, she swam mostly under water to get to the other side of the pool. Once there, she hooked her arms into the groove of the drain gully that ran around the pool's rectangle and allowed her legs to drift out in front to her. The tips of her toes appeared and she remembered that Aine had offered to paint her nails that evening. She averted her eyes and looked up at the honey-hued, praline surface of the villa's front and the tubular red roof-tiles and how they appeared pastry-pinched at the edges. She watched her friend climb out the other end and liquid sunlight fly from her slender frame. She envied Aine's figure and the money she spent on a personal trainer. Carmel was married and had no time for such luxuries; she had recently taken up Zumba in a near-by church-hall. Then she remembered how they had not rowed when she had surprised Aine checking her own texts, their second evening in the villa. She had been about to light on her but held back when she realised that her friend was staring disconsolately at the lit-up rectangle of the screen. This alarmed Carmel.

– Good God, Aine. Is there anything the matter?

The text was from Aine's partner: 'partner' not in the socio-anthropological, relationship meaning of the word, but rather in the corporate, business sense, although he and Aine had been having an affair. The message was to inform Aine that he was sticking with his wife of twelve years.

– This little break, Aine explained in a hoarse whisper. Was meant to give him time to come to a decision about us. Seems he has.

That evening they got drunk on a balcony bar overlooking Xania harbour. Aine danced to some euro-pop and Indie music that she affected, in Carmel's opinion, to recognise, all to impress a Greek youth called Costas.

– What are you doing? Carmel demanded when Costas was up at the bar getting a drink.

– I want sex, Aine replied. I'm a jilted lover and I want some love.

- You can't just go off with him. Carmel insisted. You don't know anything about him.

- Well then: I'll invite him back to the villa.

- What? So he can murder us all in our sleep? Or steal our money?

In the event, Costas was seen some time later to exit the bar with a younger Scandinavian girl. When Carmel and Aine left the bar, and despite Aine's disappointment, they were both halted in their tracks by the soft gauze of gently toned light reflected in and refracted from the gentle waters of the harbour and which seemed to lap over, envelop and appease them in the luminous and softly descending darkness of the Cretan night.

The next day, the son of the villa's owner managed to procure them a hire car, albeit one with scraped fenders and dented side-panels. Aine had a hang-over, so Carmel showed her license details and signed as designated driver. The son advised them to use the main highway to get to Falsarno beach; in his broken English he referred to it as 'the big road'.

On the way to the big road Carmel was alarmed to look in the rear view mirror and see a white van close behind, flashing its head-lights. She pulled over and the van drew alongside. The driver leaned over to his passenger side and rolled down the window.

- See what he wants, Carmel told Aine who was hesitating lowering her own window.

— What if he's a nutter?

— Well. There's two of us.

The van man had no English but he kept prodding his finger at his fuel gauge and then pointing downwards at the hire car. In his torrent of Greek, the girls could make out the word 'venzeenee' being repeated. At length, Aine saw fit to dismiss him by nodding avidly and giving him a thumbs up. When he had driven on they both got out. There was a damp patch on the surface of the parched road.

— A bloody leak, Carmel said.

Aine dabbed a finger into the puddle and brought it up to her nose.

— Well. It's not petrol, she announced.

— I hope it's not brake fluid.

— Can't be. Surely there'd be a chemical smell. There's no smell I can make out. We better find a garage.

— We should of known better from the look of the thing, Carmel declared as they got back in. It's a wreck.

They found a modest, two pump service station a couple of miles further along. The garage-owner could speak English and swiftly put their minds at ease.

— You too have this at home, he instructed them. In England.

— Ireland, Aine said.

– It is water. From the AC. This is normal.

– So, it's okay to drive then? Carmel quizzed him.

– Yes. Your AC in Ireland does this too.

Driving off again, Aine commented:

– There's a man who's obviously never been to Ireland.

Reflecting on how he'd happily given his advice for free, Carmel said:

– I can't get over how nice the Greeks are.

– Except Costas, Aine replied.

– Except him, Carmel said.

That evening they unhesitatingly relinquished the hire car, happy to spend the last two days on the island by the poolside. There they talked when they wanted to and went unbothered by the stretch of silences that interspersed their random conversations. A cloud's unexpected passage in the cobalt sky was an event. Hornets came and sipped at the pool's edge. In the evenings, swallows would skim the surface of the pool leaving soft dimples of contact in their wake. And, all the time, the aural backdrop of cicadas, like the constant turning of the key in some weird, wind-up, clockwork contraption. Aine collected a discarded, disembodied cicada wing, holding it up to the light to better regard the delicate filigree pattern of veins in its translucent surface.

Now Aine was shouting from the patio area to see if Carmel wanted a beer.

    — In a mo. I want to do a few lengths first, Carmel replied.

Assiduously, she performed ten lengths of the pool. Then, emerging, she resisted the urge to wrap her beach towel around her and hide her hips. Aine was stretched out on a canvas sun-lounger, her nose in a Nesbo. Beside her, on a small fold-away table was a can of Mythos Premium Helenic Beer. As Carmel towelled her hair, she looked up from her book and said:

    — Do you want me to go and get you a beer?

It was early afternoon but it was also their last day at the villa; the next day they would fly to Athens and after one more day, return home; to household, and office hours, and heart-ache.

    — Why not? Carmel said. Go ahead.

    — Hasn't the time flown? Aine remarked over her shoulder on the way to the kitchen. It hardly seems like any time since we were arriving.

They had rowed within half an hour of arriving at Irakleio's Airport of St. Nicholas. The taxis were on strike and there were no hire cars to be had. The few passengers that had been on the flight with them were to be seen strung out at different intervals along the dusty road to town, a desperate band of tourist refugees. In 40 degree heat, the girls trundled their valises along behind them until eventually Aine insisted on stopping.

    — We're going to miss the coach to Xania, Carmel warned.

    — Fuck the coach to Xania, Aine seethed. I'm putting sun-screen on.

She proceeded to zip open side pouches and pockets in search of her factor 25.

    — You should wear a hat like me, Carmel grumbled. And not worry about your hair so much.

What interrupted this exchange was the sudden appearance of a local service bus which pulled up although they were near no designated bus stop. Gratefully they bundled and blundered their way on board. Then there was the tomfoolery of trying to get tickets. They were both seasoned travellers and between them could express themselves confidently with a happy multitude of imperfections in a wide range of languages. When the driver pulled up at a kiosk, Aine understood enough to dismount and purchase two tickets. These she tried to press into the driver's hand, much to the polite amusement of the local passengers who sat audience-like and unworried by any delay to their journey. Carmel caught on:

    — Punch them, she shouted above the din of the engine. In that machine there. You've got to date-stamp them.

The bus went quiet as it passed a picket line of pro-testing taxi-drivers. They were assembled around the burnt carcasses of two cars. To their experienced eyes the wrecks did not resemble riot damage nor barri-cading. Later they learned that two taxi men had im-molated their own vehicles in protest at the Greek government's plan to open up the industry with new licensing laws.

The bus driver got them to the coach station in plenty of time. It was a two hour journey along the island to Xania. Carmel attempted to look out and take in the dusty, sun-scorched hills on one side and the glittering turquoise on the other; but after the enforced hike in the heat she soon drowsed and woke only when the coach was manoeuvring dexter-ously through the tight and bumpy streets of central Xania. Then they were trundling again, over broken kerb stones and loose paving. A second service bus got them to the villa.

*

There was something extra for the tourists in Syn-tagma Square that year. The 'Indignants' had set up a tent city outside the metro station and opposite the Hellenic Parliament. It was the final days of Papan-dreou's Government. Through severe austerity meas-ures, ministers had been trying to win support for more financial aid from an international community that had begun increasingly to doubt Athens' desire to modernise itself. At the tomb of the Unknown Soldier, the fancy dressed Presidential Guards were still pulling a crowd; Carmel and Aine among them.

– They're called 'Evzoni', Aine was reading from her guide. A name derived from Homer's Iliad, it seems.

– Look, Carmel interrupted. They're moving.

They resembled costumed, cantilevered automatons only, in that heat, their tunics darkened quickly with their body moisture. At intervals, a third officer, in modern garb, would come forward and dab their faces with a cloth and adjust aspects of their uniforms. He also seemed to lean in close and talk intently to them though it was hard to be sure of this as he had his back to the tourists.

– That poor fellow on the right looks as if he's going to topple any minute, Carmel said.

– The whole country looks as if it could topple any minute, Aine observed.

Around them, there were banners stretched from lamp-posts, posters affixed to walls. On their way into the Plaka area, they passed a phalanx of police tenders. They were able to peer into the interior of one or two; in one, young officers were playing cards, a couple in another played backgammon. The girls had seen it all before.

— They're gearing up for action, Carmel said to Aine in the restaurant they had been inveigled into entering by a friendly but persuasive waiter.

In her mind's eye she saw again her father who had not been a particularly politicised person, but who, on that day, felt impelled, along with his neighbours to attend the huge protest march. She could see him with his raincoat draped across his arm, disappearing through the ranks of soldiers that had flooded the town that morning in anticipation of trouble though, in the event, the mass demonstration was carried off in a solemn and dignified fashion. No rioting had ensued.

— Stop it, Aine interrupted as if she could read her friend's mind. It's all ancient history now. It's our last evening: let's enjoy a good farewell meal.

The restaurant was called the Agora restaurant as it sat alongside the ruins of the original Agora which had once been a place of public meetings and mass assemblies in the middle of Athens. In the growing dark, above them, on the outcrop of the Acropolis, the spot lights came on, illuminating the several columns of the Parthenon.

Carmel had been right though.

On the day they arrived back in Belfast, the Greek police tooled-up, visor-ed faces, snapped on helmets, hefted shields and, wielding batons, cleaned out Syntagma Square. Carmel watched the scenes with her husband that evening on the television news; yet, despite the many frenetic camera angles on the action, she was not able to make out if the ornamental, presidential guards remained in situ throughout.

The Gardens of Suburbia

They had no idea their neighbour was a writer until the invitation to the book launch was handed to them, one late summer afternoon, across the fence. He'd been weeding and turning the soil around some rose bushes when, seeing them come out, he had gone in to fetch the glossy invitation.

— Now don't feel you have to go, he assured them. It'd be good to see you there. The publisher usually supplies a nice glass of wine. Or two.

Laura said:
— Not for me.
— No indeed, he agreed. You'll have your own 'work of art' soon enough, he joked with her.

That evening, Bob Googled their neighbour.
— We should have known he was a writer, he said to the screen. I'm sure I've heard his name somewhere.

    — But have you read any of his stuff? Laura asked coming up and laying a hand on his shoulder and looking at the monitor.

    — No. You? After all, you're the one who did English A level, he added.

Leaning forward, Laura examined the list of publications. None of the titles were familiar.

    — Let's order one, she suggested.

There was an offer of next day delivery for orders of over £25, so they clicked his most recent title, 'The Big Simulacrum and Other Stories', along with two DVDs, into the basket and proceeded to checkout.

    Next evening, Bob spotted the copy on the dresser in the kitchen and after glancing at the cover he skimmed the blurb information at the back. Laura however, took the book with her to bed. The following night, when Bob came up to bed, she was able to leaf through pages and read out passages to him that had impressed her.

    — I can't believe we have a famous writer living beside us, she enthused.

    — I wonder if it adds anything to the value of the house, Bob said.

She ignored this and turned to a new story.

It had been shortly after their moving into the house that the neighbour had volunteered the information about his habit of sitting in his garden at night.

– Not every night, he added. Really just at week-ends. But just so as you know and don't go out some night into your garden and get a shock.

This was before they knew he wrote. Bob thought him strange. Laura thought him lonely; a theory confirmed by their neighbour on the other side, who revealed how the writer had lost his wife two years previously. Now, reading his stories, it seemed even more natural for him to sit outside.

One story made Laura reflective and heavy with thought. Another had her reaching for her dictionary. A third one turned her on – Bob *was* taken by surprise. All made her curious. At first, she merely glanced in the direction of the next door garden, on her way up to bed; but before long, and almost without realising it, she had grown more attentive, more alert to any shift or movement she could detect in the evening twilight. Again unconsciously, she quickly gathered that there were two viable viewpoints of the neighbour's garden; one from the landing window, the other, a more oblique angle offered by the window in the return room at the very back of the house. And, on a few occasions, her curiosity was repaid with slight sightings of him sitting in the garden. On one occasion, a storm bucked and roared in their gardens making the trees at the bottom dip and bend, the wind contorting wildly to disentangle itself from the clinging foliage; and she realised she could make him out sitting in the midst of this in a coat and woolly cap. Another night, all was calm and she could see him simply sitting there. She could not accuse him of gazing on her house as he sat facing the bottom of his garden.

— But what does he do? Bob enquired.

— I think he must write, she surmised.

— What! In the dark, he scoffed.

— In his head, she half scowled at him. In the dark.

She had this picture of him sitting there watching bat flight overhead, or night fall, or trees flail in the wind, and, all the time, words forming in his head. There was a mist the third time she saw him. And something drew her face closer to the pane so that as she peered out she allowed herself to be suddenly startled by either an actual or imagined – she could not, even later, decide which – movement, or intimation of a movement, as if he was about to turn suddenly and look directly up at her and, so powerful was this impression, she jumped backwards, despite her condition, bumping loudly into the landing wall in an effort to evade detection.

— Laura? Are you all right? Bob called up concerned from the kitchen.

For the next couple of days, Laura puzzled as to what had made her start so. Even within the shifting billow of the mist, there had been a residue of light in the garden, refracted perhaps from off the low cloud, even emanating from the flower beds themselves or issuing in a confluent glow from all the television sets burning in darkened rooms up and down the avenue around them, and in this low wattage illumination she had discerned, made out, something, not new perhaps nor even unusual, only, it somehow came to her: extra to what - again without her realising she had begun to do so - she regarded as the natural composition of his sitting there in the garden at night. Then, this merest impression grew suddenly clear to her, woke her up in fact, very early one morning so that, emerging further from her slumber she almost saw it: the presence, the extra element to the scene. And it made her sit up in the bed as it struck her at last what she had intuited more than seen, sensed more than clearly delineated from her sight line on the landing: he had not been on his own, that night, in the garden; there had been another figure with him in the mist.

There was a burley door-man on the door of the bookshop for the launch. He hardly glanced at the invitation that Laura dutifully produced for him. The noise of laughter and clinkage came from within and they could make out vague, bobbing shapes through the display windows. On entering, a waitress, weaving in and out of these guests, spotted their arrival and made her way over to them with a drinks tray. Laura took an orange juice, Bob enquired after a beer but had to settle for a glass of red wine. They didn't immediately spot their neighbour, but publicity stills of him adorned the front of the shop where his new book was on display. Eagerly, Laura lifted a copy.

— It's a bit small, Bob whispered. How much is it?

Laura turned the book around and then lifted the fly-leaf and read £12.99.

— That's a bit steep, Bob said. Given the size of it.

Laura looked at him.

— What? He protested. I'm just saying it's not War and Peace; that's all. Make sure he signs it.

— You both made it. Excellent. The neighbour was suddenly at their side.

— Of course we did, Laura exclaimed. Though we are a wee bit out of our depth, she confessed, nodding at the throng around her.

— Not a bit of it, he insisted. I'll introduce you to some nice people later. Right now I've got to talk to the local press. It's all go.

They stood stiffly with their copy of the book and looked around them. They recognised a famous playwright; and some local names off the radio and television. They also spotted some other neighbours and nodded tentatively at them. The neighbour from the other side came over and asked Laura how she was.

– Not long now. By the looks of it. It'll be great to have children in the avenue again. I'm afraid we've all grown so old and boring, she said.

– Well, you can't call this boring, Laura answered, waving in general around her. It's like having a celebrity living beside us.

– He'd hate you calling him a celebrity, the woman warned her.

Laura knew what she meant; she recalled that time talking to him across the fence and asking him if he was looking forward to the launch. His reply had been:

– You spend months – maybe years – working away on your own; shut up in your study; burning the midnight oil. It can be a lonely business. And then, suddenly, you're expected to jump up in front of the public and make a spectacle of yourself; give interviews, have your photograph taken. It's a bit disconcerting.

Remembering this and suddenly finding him looking directly over at her, across the shop floor, she mouthed 'Good Luck' to him and he smiled in reply and nodded as if to indicate he understood. The manager of the bookshop was calling for order and making a joke about asking so many poets and writers to be silent. The guest speaker was not the famous playwright but his wife; the manager introduced her as a professor of literature, distinguished critic and commentator. Laura recognised her off some late night arts panels. Out of the corner of her eye, she saw Bob get the waitress' attention and a second glass of wine.

The Professor's speech was short but heart-felt; when she alluded to the writer's bereavement, the silent audience seemed to fall even more silent and when she read a particularly moving extract, some guests dabbed discreetly at their eyes or shifted slightly where they stood; Laura felt herself well up. Yet, the speaker declared, in the end, the beauty of the book was its affirmation of life; the 'urging', as she put it, to move on; to embrace life.

Their neighbour indicated how gratified he was that the Professor had detected such positive elements in the book.

– As anyone who's read my work will know: I don't really do happy. Yet it was important to me that this book was not all doom and gloom. That's not to say it wasn't a struggle to find the energy or the motivation to complete it; that I did find the necessary strength is due in no small part to the support and love of friends and colleagues. And here he named a number of people.

He then lifted a copy of the novel and began to leaf through it for an extract to read. As he did so, he continued to address the gathering:

– Now: having said all that, it hasn't escaped people's notice how slim the novel actually is. And, in this time of credit crunch and economic downturn, £12.99 does seem a bit steep.

Laura turned and glared at Bob. He stared wide-eyed at her, his face already red with the wine and the heat in the shop.

– My only defence is that I've packed so much into this short novel that, to really appreciate it, you would have to read it a second time. Well, that is except for pages 98, 67 and the bottom half of 34, he added. So, you see, it's really 214 pages long, not 107. A bargain!

This received loud laughter all around and then he had the audience spell-bound as he read a passage from the book. Afterwards, there was so long a line of people wanting to get their copies signed that Laura said she had to go; they would have to get theirs signed at a more convenient time.

The baby arrived two days later. They had been more secure with a boy's name but had difficulty agreeing one for the baby girl; so for a few days she was just called 'baby'.

In the maternity unit, the nurses were a great support and comfort. The day Bob came to drive mother and daughter home, Laura felt a sense of panic. When they carried 'baby' into the house, she was fast asleep. They set the carry-cot down gently on the living room carpet; Bob had lit the fire. Both sat down looking alternately at the cot then up at one another and main-

tained a stunned silence until eventually Laura whispered:

— What are we going to do if she wakes up?

— I have no idea, Bob conceded and then he
grinned at her.

So it was some time before Laura got time or energy
to read the neighbour's novel. The weather was wet
and cold anyway and, although she rarely peered out
the windows now, she was sure the rain kept him indoors.

Eventually, the spring came and one day, as she
was hanging washing out on the rotary clothes line, he
appeared around the corner of his house with a bag
of compost balanced on his right shoulder. He saw
her and asked after her health and the baby's.

— I hope she doesn't keep you awake at night,
Laura said.

— I haven't heard a thing, he assured her.

— Anyway, I read your book, she plainly told him.

— Ah, he responded. You shouldn't be wasting
your time on such rubbish.

— It's not rubbish, she insisted. And you know it's
not; so don't say it.

He laughed at her rebuke and said:

— Well. Thank you.

— I can't say I understood every page, she confessed. But I did enjoy it.

He thanked her again and bent to pick up the compost when she delayed him with a further admission:

— I also re-read those pages.

He straightened up again and looked at her inquisitively.

— What pages? He asked.

— The ones you said not to re-read.

— Whatever for? He looked a little shocked. Do you always do what you're told not to?

— I'm right then, she exclaimed.

— I don't follow.

— There's something hidden in those pages. Like a code or something. That's why you mentioned them.

— I'm not Dan Brown, he retorted and she suddenly felt she had offended him.

— I'm sorry, she said. I'm mad in the head. 'Hormones', Bob maintains. Forget what I said.

As she turned back to the clothes basket, it was his turn to delay her.

— Just out of interest: did you find anything?

She looked at him while a new thought formed in her head and her tone was sharp when she said:

— Now you're just trying to make fun of me.

— No, he hastened to assure her. I'm fascinated. Maybe I put something in subconsciously. Without realising it.

She studied him closely, all the time weighing up this last statement. At last she relented and revealed what she thought she had discovered:

    — I could only find something on the half page you mentioned.

    — Page 34, if I remember rightly.

    — That's correct, she said. The first letter of each sentence in the paragraph spells the name 'Jenny'.

    — An acrostic, he said.

    — I've only ever seen them in poetry, she went on. Then, after a pause, she asked the question: Was that your wife's name?

He returned her look and then shook his head.

    — Afraid not. My wife's name was Cynthia. So you see: there is no code. Without a further word, he hefted the bag of compost and disappeared into his garden shed leaving her standing there with a handful of babygros and clothes pegs.

She did not dare go near the windows overlooking his garden after this exchange. She barely glanced at her own pale reflection as she went quickly upstairs and along the landing in her long night gown. She felt she wanted to avoid him at least for the next couple of days, in which time, he would hopefully forget her foolishness. However, Bob met him as he pulled into his driveway one evening. When he came into the house and on into the kitchen, he announced that the neighbour had invited them to a party.

    — Not this weekend but the following. We've nothing on, do we?

    — What about the baby?

    — He said to bring her. Anyway, if needs be we can take turns minding her. It's only next door after all.

There were guests in the garden next door.

    Laura was back at the landing window. She could see their vague forms strolling about the garden. She could hear the murmur of voices and music issuing from the back of the house; she recognised Vampire Weekend's first album playing on the sound-system.

    Bob had opted to do first watch and when he came out from checking on the baby he was startled to find Laura still standing on the landing.

    — Go on, he urged, adding: It's not like you to be shy.

The neighbour's front door was opened. The music had changed to Arcade Fire's 'The Suburbs'. Laura could see down the hall to the back of the house; she nodded at people as she made her way along to the kitchen where she had spied the host opening wine. He held the bottle she had brought up into the candle light, the better to appraise the label and, admiring her choice, placed it along with others on the counter.

– We'll enjoy that one in a wee while, he assured her. In the mean-time, try this- He stopped himself suddenly in mid-pour of a large goblet of red wine.

– If that's okay of course. I mean: you're not – well, obviously you're not driving – but maybe you're, you know, breast-feeding or something? I've got fizzy water if you prefer. Or I can put the kettle on.

– It's okay, Laura interjected, laughing at his consternation and relieved that no awkwardness seemed to hang over from their last exchange.

– Come out to the garden, he invited her. I'm bringing this to the 'Prof', he said indicating another glass of wine he held. You remember her: she spoke at the book launch. You've got to meet her, he added.

Laura followed him out to the patio and marvelled at the garden. There was the merest blade of a moon in the sky but the garden was illuminated anyway by an array of outdoor lighting: festoon lights were strung around the roof and windows of the garden shed; replica oil lamps and storm lanterns and miners' lanterns sheltered candles from the slight, light breeze, as did glass jar votive tea-light holders and bamboo spear lanterns; there were also some solar spike lights staked in among the shrubbery and flowers. Some of the candles were aromatic and mingled their fragrance with the natural scents emanating from the patio tubs filled with evening primrose, tobacco plants and the luminous, moth friendly silver ghost; all unfurling their petals now that it was twilight. The tall elegant woman turned around as they emerged onto the patio and smiled.

– Have you met our distinguished Professor? he asked Laura.

– He introduces me like that to everyone, she mildly chided the neighbour. Please, she insisted: Call me Jenny.

– Oh, Laura said; and in all that candle-light she could still see the look of concern cross the woman's face.

– Are you all right? She enquired, placing a hand on Laura's arm. You look like you've seen a ghost.

At that very moment the fluorescent strip lights came on in Laura's own kitchen next door; the darkness seemed to flinch and shrink down the garden, which was overgrown and unkempt what with them really only having moved in and the baby and what not; and she could picture Bob in the kitchen making up the bottles for the night feed, assiduously measuring out the powdered formula, boiling the water, shaking the mixture; placing the bottles upright in the fridge.

– Maybe you should go back inside the house, the neighbour was suggesting to her.

– No, she replied, and she looked him straight in the face. I think I'll be fine now.

Though what she really thought was: if she could only vault the fence, she would.

Upstairs

   — I am taking us, she informed him, to a house in the country that is temporarily vacant. And to which I have the key.

Although she was driving, it sounded as if she was reading from a written statement and he looked at her. She returned his look before redirecting her attention to the winding country road they were on.

   — It's fine by me, he said at length.

Around a bend she had to slow and go down gears and trundle along behind a tractor for half a mile until it turned into a corn-field. He heard her say, Come on, come on, beneath her breath.

They had left the motorway some miles back. Looking past her profile across the fields, he could see motorway traffic running parallel to them: vans and lorries taking freight out from or into the city, reps speeding to represent their businesses, solicitors their clients; ambulances with or without flashing lights, police patrol cars; the flux and flow of any mid-week, working day. Only that day she wore a skirt. She rarely did at work, and now, as she drove along, she could sense his discreet and intermittent glances down.

She let him look.

They passed a country church with its manicured cemetery alongside and then the manse and then they drove on through a small village. It had been a 'best kept' village once and there were bright flower baskets suspended from lamp posts and archways and gable ends and no inhabitants in sight. People would be at work.

— Not far now, she asserted.

The house she intended had the indent of a private lay-by at its front to allow a car to park safely off the road. She pulled in here and turning off the engine she indicated the house.

— There it is, she declared.

— It's very nice, he said. Very rustic.

They sat a while like that, gazing out the passenger side, taking in the house and its small garden.

— Shall we go in then? she said at length.

— Of course, he agreed.

Getting out, she reached in behind the driver's seat and pulled out a large, oversized hand bag before locking the car and preceding him to the garden gate. He followed her along the small path to the front door. An ornamental, ceramic squirrel was affixed in frozen descent to the porch. A lion shaped door knocker gazed at them. He waited as she rummaged in the hand bag and eventually located a bunch of keys from which she skilfully selected the Yale one which gave them access.

– Quickly, she said aloud. I have to turn the alarm off.

She flipped open the box on the hall wall and deftly typed in the password and the tiny red light went green and a small electrical humming ceased. They stood in silence in the hall.

– Come on, she said.

She led the way down the hall and in though a door into a kitchen; once through the door, he could see that the room convexed out into a conservatory extension with a fine view of a small, walled garden.

– A beautiful garden, he commented, walking on into the conservatory. A beautiful house, in fact, he said, surveying his surroundings. His eye approved the prints and pictures on the walls.

His comment acted like some prompt for she suddenly was looking studiously at the bunch of keys again, in her hand. This time she levered up a longer key which she went and inserted in the lock in the back door. Swinging open the door she said to him:

– Wait till you see this.

They went out into the well maintained, mature garden and stepped onto the springy surface of the lawn. Stopping, she raised a finger in the air, inviting him to listen:

    – Do you hear it?

He strained to hear something. In the distance there was some farm machinery; a bailer he thought. Closer, he could make out the un-oiled winch and pulley sound a robin makes. If you see one robin, there's always two, his gardening uncle used to maintain; they're very faithful.

    – Do you not hear it? Come closer.

They stepped further down towards the wall at the bottom of the garden and then he could make out the small, low frequency current in the air between them, emitting from some source, out of sight, beyond the brickwork.

    – A river, he declared.

    – Yes, she exclaimed with pleasure. A river at the bottom of the garden. How cool is that?

    – "I often wished that I had clear," he was suddenly trying to remember aloud. "For life, six hundred pounds a year/A handsome house to lodge a friend/A river at my garden's end."

    – That's pretty, she responded. Who is it?

    – Swift, he replied. Jonathan Swift.

She shook her head in light-hearted exasperation at the levels of learning he would sometimes demonstrate. As she did so, he spotted the blue, wooden door, recessed into the wall and went and tried it. It wouldn't give.

— I'm not sure if any of these keys will open it, she said. I think they're all for the house.

— It doesn't matter, he said. He walked back to where she was standing and all the time the thought was forming until he said:

— I wonder if you can see the river from the bedroom.

At this they turned around and regarded the rear of the house. Their eyes were drawn to the upstairs window.

— It must be lovely to wake up to and look out at, she mused.

Her statement hung between them in the air as they stood on in the garden, looking upwards and the river flowed along out of sight behind the wall. At length, she broke their reverie:

— Come on: let's go back indoors.

They returned to the house and she made sure to lock the back door again. Then she felt prompted to suggest:

— I know. We can have a cup of tea. Or coffee, if you prefer.

— I can't do this, he suddenly announced. I'm so sorry.

She froze at the fridge. Then:

— There's no milk anyway, she said, closing over the fridge door.

The house's absent owner was a collector of fridge magnets; a 'star-crossed lovers' one, from the Globe gift shop, stood suddenly and prominently out to her.

— Let's go somewhere and get a coffee, she said, gathering up her oversized hand bag and the bunch of keys and making, without waiting for him, for the front door.

In this little land, you can be in country-side one minute and concrete the next. Through the spool and con-volutions of two large roundabouts, they eventually found a shopping complex and parked in the Tesco's carpark. They had hardly exchanged two words during this second, shorter drive.

They entered the store and followed the arrows to an over bright café section where they got two cappuccinos. Neither wanted anything to eat. They carried their cups to a table overlooking the aisles of shuf-fling shoppers, ageing among the shelves of wares and produce. They shared the café with two men talking urgently in suits and loosened ties; and, by herself, a middle aged woman sitting in the company of a cream scone and tea-pot.

Indicating the suits, she murmured:

— I wonder what's got them all hot and both-ered.

— Worries of the world, looks like, he replied.

That day the FTSE 100 would finish down 2.2% at 5421 after an initial fall of 5% while the German Dax and French CAC were due to remain 5% down at the close. The Dow Jones index of US companies would at one stage fall more than 300 points before a slight recovery.

They looked to their left then and watched as the woman took up a knife and determinedly cut the scone in two and began to trowel jam and cream onto the severed ends.

— There goes this week's weight watchers, she said.

— I'm sorry, he suddenly said again. I wanted to. I mean it's not you. It's me.

— That's all right, she hushed him. I'm not sure I could have either.

They gazed down at their cups that sat inches apart on the Formica surface of the table.

She drove him home, dropping him a few doors from his house. Slipping off his seat-belt and climb-ing out, she reminded him not to forget his brief-case. He reached in behind the passenger seat to retrieve it.

He was shocked to see his wife's car in the driveway at that hour. Lois was startled too in the hall-way when he turned the key in the front door, puzzled by his early and unexpected return.

— What are you doing home this early? she enquired. I thought your meeting was an all-day affair.

— It ended earlier than expected, he replied. What are you doing home? Is something wrong?

— It's alright, she assured him. Lily across the street contacted work to say she had seen someone suspicious going round the back of the house. I got covered at work and came straight home to check.

Lily was the kindly widow who kept an eye out for anything untoward happening in the neighbourhood. There had been a spate of break-ins.

— Good God, he exclaimed. Who was it?

— The gas man. Seems someone okayed this afternoon for him to come and service the boiler. Wasn't me.

It suddenly struck him that he had agreed the time, the previous week as he had arranged in his work diary to be working from home on that day.

— It was me. I completely forgot, he apologised. I've had a lot on my mind of late.

— Well. No harm done. At least we know not much gets past Lily, she said.

He followed Lois out into the kitchen where she suddenly stopped and turned to him.

— Listen, she said.

For the second time that day, he stood and strained to hear something; there was no river at the bottom of his garden. Finally he gave up and said:

— What? I can't hear anything.

— Exactly, she replied. The kids'll not be home for another hour.

At this remark, he looked closely at her. He raised his eyebrows.

— And...? He enquired.

— Well. It just struck me: when was the last time we did it on a week-day? In the middle of the afternoon.

— Don't you have to get back to work?

Lois returned his look and slowly shook her head; whereupon she turned and proceeded back down the hallway towards the bottom of the stairs. After a moment, he followed her, halting only to bend down for his briefcase where he'd left it in the hall to take up to the study.

— Forget the bloody briefcase, she demanded.

Then, seeing the slightly startled look on her husband's face, Lois reached out and, taking one of his hands, she began gently but firmly to lead him up the stairs.

The Widow

"'Excuse me," he said. "I've come to the wrong door."
"I wish that were true, she said, "but death makes no
mistakes."
From 'Maria dos Prazeres' by Gabriel García
Márquez.

1.

He had come at last.

She had been standing in her front room when his
car appeared. She did not know it was his car, as she
had not seen him for some years, but had looked up
and watched it anyway. For some time she had been
standing in the middle of the room looking over at
the library book on the mantle piece. The room which
had been so recently crowded now yawned spaciously
about her and she stood a little lost, looking at the
library book. Minutes before she had determined to go
into the room and pick it up and put it in her bag; then
the sight of her husband's thick, leather book mark,
halted her advance. It had the legend 'fatto in Toscana'
skilfully tooled into its fragrant surface and was clearly

visible, inserted at a mid-way mark in the white pith of the book; and it transfixed her. Her granddaughter had bought light metallic folding seats from Ikea to fill this room and the TV room where they had laid him out. Now the seats were all removed and the front room was as large and empty as the whole house. She was standing there and the car appeared and distracted her, allowing her to look away and move over to the window.

He had parked a couple of houses down, at the opposite kerb, as if at a discreet distance. There was plenty of space outside her own house as she had quickly learned to reverse the car the way her husband would into the narrow drive-way. This was a precaution, given the young families that had moved in around them and the toddlers and children that spilled out of the people carriers and four by fours: it was safer to reverse into the smaller space rather than lurch outwards into the avenue. Idly, she watched as he hauled himself out of the driver's seat with as much dignity as his body would allow; only when he straightened up did she recognise him. The way he surveyed the house fronts told her he was forgetful of where she actually lived and she almost rapped the window. Then he seemed to get his bearings and turned and looked directly at her. She was seventy and still light on her feet, for she stepped smartly away from the bay window, back into the centre of the room and held her breath.

Apart from a coat, she was dressed to go out. With great relief she felt she was not as unpresentable as she fancied she would have been if he had caught her in her housework clothes or bathrobe. House work had begun to help her through the day; she knew all about the wheelie bins now and which one was which and when to put them out. She had even begun to trundle the young-couple-next-door's bins back up their drive when emptied and before they got back from work. She had found out where the stop cock was, in case the winter was as harsh as the one just past. But oh: the book. She left it where it was and walked to the front door and went out to meet him.

He was crossing the road and he looked up and saw her there and stopped; then he raised his right hand in the air. Even at that little distance, raising their voices to each other seemed inappropriate, so she simply nodded her head and he came on then and spoke only when he was in the drive-way:

— Lilly, he said. I am so sorry. I was not able to make the funeral.

— Well, she said, regarding a moment and then accepting the formal hand shake he offered her. You are here now.

What she really wanted to say was: "I looked for you every time the doorbell rang; or when I heard voices in the hall. I looked for you among the neighbours who came with their sandwiches in tin foil and boxes of biscuits; I looked for you among his friends, the members of the rambling club he belonged to, the ecumenical group he was secretary of; the book club and those he played golf with. I looked for you among the clergy: those ministers and priests; among the mourners in the chapel. Even at the grave-side!"

— Come inside, she said.

He followed her into the house. He had a light weatherproof on and she took it for him and draped it over the newel post at the bottom of the stairs. She avoided the front room and led him, instead, down the hall and into the kitchen with its conservatory extension and view of the garden. She noticed that the sun was out.

— I hear it was very sudden. That he did not suffer, he said, lowering himself with a slight grimace into a chair at the kitchen table.

— Sudden, she confirmed.

They had just finished a five mile hike and were in a café. He had gone to keep a table and when the others looked round he was slumped peacefully in a seat. One of the number was a retired doctor who worked on him. The ambulance came within five minutes it seems; but it was all over by then.

He sat and took this in and simply shook his head.

— Out walking, he reflected. It is not a bad way to go.

    — I am tired of people saying that, she replied and he looked up at her.

She stood leaning against one of the kitchen's work surfaces with her arms folded and returned his look with a frown. On entering, she had automatically clicked on the kettle and it began to rev up noisily behind her, so she almost did not hear him say:

    — I could not come. It did not feel right.

    — I know, she said.

She turned away and busied herself making him a cup of tea, knowing, without having to ask, that he did not need milk nor want sugar. Her hand trembled as she brought it over to him and seeing this he half rose to take the cup securely from her; their fingers touched.

    — Watch. It is hot, she warned.

    — I wanted to come, he replied. For you.

She moved back across the kitchen and proceeded to make herself a coffee.

    — There is no point offering you a biscuit or a piece of cake. I have enough biscuits to last me I do not know how long.

    — Not a sweet person, he pattered.

    — Sweet enough, she rapped back.

    — You look tired, he said.

    — Old?

– We are all old. But no. You just look tired. It is understandable I expect.

She sat down at the table opposite him like one of Cezanne's card players.

– You look well, she told him. Then she could not stop herself from checking:

– I hope *you* are looking after yourself: your blood pressure. Cholesterol.

– Do not worry. Jocelyn makes sure I go for check ups.

– And how is Jocelyn?

– She is well. Still playing badminton. She sends her love.

She looked over at him at this remark.

– She knows you are here then?

– I told her I was coming.

She nodded and took a sip of her coffee.

– I am still playing tennis, she said.

– Why would you not be? He replied.

There was a soft, yellow detonation of a bum-bee against the window, as if someone was tapping for attention and the house all of a sudden fell silent around them. A lawn was being mowed in the neighbourhood and as it was a weekday they could only assume it was someone's paid gardener; or an active retired person. A clock ticked somewhere, audible but unseen.

— I keep meaning to turn the radio on, she said. Dispel the silence.

— They say this is the most terrible time; after all the visits have stopped.

— I keep expecting him to just walk in. With the paper or some bit of gossip from a neighbour.

They sat and cast glances up the hallway. They listened to see if any doors would open or floor boards creak, or risers on the stair case; if a familiar voice would suddenly call to them. Then he caught her eye and she said:

— I miss him, you know.

He nodded and cleared his throat and said nothing; and she thought:

"How wise you are to just nod. To clear your throat in that uncertain manner of yours and know not to say anything; not: Of course you miss him or: Why would you not miss him? or: What a good man he was; though all these things are true; but not for you to say them. How good you are to know this and shift the way you do in your chair and sip your tea."

As she studied his tanned and weathered face, creased like a nautical chart, an idea sprang into her head and she almost shouted out:

— You are still not surfing are you?

He laughed at the incredulousness.

— Paddling, he put it. I still paddle out once in a while and watch the young ones. It is crowded out there nowadays. I catch the odd wave.

— I can only imagine what you look like in a wet-suit.

— I will have you know I still cut a fine figure, he protested.

They laughed at little more at this and for a moment there was a brief respite from the invisible clock and the empty weight of the heavy house. Then he spoke again:

— Your daughter lives nearby. Does she not?

— Just around the corner. And her two daughters are home now from university. Both working. Some-one calls nearly every evening. I am alright in that de-partment.

— Both working, he mused. God. We are getting old.

— You are wearing well, she insisted. Still a great head of hair.

He raked at his hair with the fingers of one hand.

— White, he said. Not even grey anymore. You have not changed though. Still beautiful.

— Thank you, she replied.

What she really meant was: "How I hunger for you. How I have to fight even now to keep from reaching over and touching you; and yet all you could do when you arrived was hold out your hand. Not even a hug when I've had strangers I have not even met before put their arms around me these past weeks and yet all you could do was offer to shake my hand, damn you."

She started when she realised he was staring at her.

— It would not have been right, he insisted. And when she did not reply he believed it was necessary to speak some more as clear hearing could no longer be taken for granted: To have come, I mean.

— I know what you mean, she reproached him. Although I am sure it would have been alright. Who would have minded?

Thinking: "Why would it not have been right? I would not have cared what anyone thought; I would not have cared if anyone had raised an eyebrow or an objection; do you not know that?" and then she recollected how weak he could be.

By then the tea cup was empty and sat on the table between them and she lifted his cup and got up and placed it in the sink. She briefly ran the tap and heard him get up behind her. He was preparing to leave and she turned suddenly and said:

— I have an email, now. Let me write it down for you.

She went to the dresser and pulled open one of the little pharmacy drawers. She lifted out a block of post-its and a pen and scribbled the address down. She gave it to him.

— Stay in touch, she said.

He took the post-it and looked briefly at it before taking out his wallet and slotting it in between his license and bank cards.

— Of course, he assured her.

"You do not mean to," she thought.

At the front door a sharp wind had started to blow, bringing the tang of sea air from the docks. The house was north facing; the sun and any warmth were in the back garden.

— Do you go on in, he urged her. It is too cold to be standing out.

Again, he held out his hand; but this time she reached for it with her left hand and held his as one would a child's when crossing the road. Holding him this way, she gently pulled him to her and kissed him. Only on the cheek; however, she saw that he was still a little alarmed and so she let him go.

"You smell just like you," she thought but she did not say this to him.

From inside the front room, she watched him go to his car. He looked around and this time she did not slink back out of sight, seventy and still light on her feet. She waved this time only to realise that he could not see her after all.

At last, she took up the hard back, library book and let it fall open at the book mark which she lifted up and held a little distance from her nose. She breathed in the fond pungency of the well worn strip of leather. Then she looked at the opened book. A chapter came to an end on the left hand page; this would be where her husband had interrupted his reading, his last evening on earth. So she let her eye linger on the text, on what would have been the last page for him. Lightly she brushed her fingers over the surface of the page, tracing where one of his last touches would have been.

Then, closing the book, she went to get her coat and car keys. She would go to the library before the rush hour traffic began, and maybe call in with her daughter on the way back.

2.

She was about to mount the ladder when she heard the front door bell and not wanting to track dirt through the house she came at her visitor by way of the gable side of the house. In such a way she outflanked Clinton, one of her late husband's walking companions. He stood oblivious to her, concentrating as he was on the front door, no doubt straining to hear if someone was within. He was dressed for walking, with a back pack tightly belted around his midriff and a sturdy pair of boots on his feet. She wore an old pair of her husband's for gardening, even though they were a size too big. She figured that if she was to call to him now, or approach him from this blind side, she risked giving him a start; so, instead, she withdrew back around the corner of the house and called out:

— Yes. I'm just coming. Who is it?

She affected surprise as she reappeared to find Clinton standing facing her.

— It's just me, he said. I hope I'm not disturbing you.

— Not at all, she assured him. In fact you're giving me an excuse to take a break: I'm around the back doing some gardening. Come on around this way.

Clinton followed her past the three wheelie bins and in through a wooden gate into the garden where a hoe was stuck standard-like in one flower bed, secateurs were splayed open on the lawn and the ladder stood expectantly against the back wall.

— I see you're keeping busy, he observed.

— The garden never stops, she said.

Clinton undid the strap from around his waist and shucked off the pack; he set it on the flagstone surface of the small patio area and lowered himself into a garden seat.

— I take it you've come on foot.

— Naturally, he stated. Traffic's mad anyway; it's almost quicker walking.

— Let me get these off, she said, indicating her boots. And I'll go and make some tea.

Clinton watched as she genuflected and undid the long laces of first one and then the other boot; as she undid the second lace, strands of her long hair came loose and draped down around her. Upright again, she kicked off the boots and attempted to talk to him with a couple of hair clips between her teeth which she used to pin her hair back up. He could make out what she was asking him and answered:

— Tea would be just fine.

Despite some dire predictions to the contrary, visitors had kept calling although the visits were less and less frequent. Nevertheless, she had now a routine whereby it was no time at all before she had the garden table set, the tea made and cake cut and placed on a serving plate. She had also acquired a proficiency with which to field the mandatory inquisition as to how she was coping. This topic out of the way, she sat and realised that Clinton had something else on his mind: an invitation. Telling him that he was looking fit and well facilitated him raising the subject:

— It's the walking, he explained. It's so good for you; which is partly why I'm here.

— Oh? She replied glancing sideways at him.

— A couple of us in the rambling club were discussing it and, what with poor Bill gone (God rest him), we obviously have a bit of a vacancy and… well, I suggested you.

— A vacancy? I didn't think there was a waiting list, she said.

— Well. Not an official one; we just thought you might want to become a member.

There was a brief silence as if she was weighing the proposition; Clinton thought to lessen the tension by saying:

— You've already got the boots.

Walking was not her thing; not the rambling, hiking type. She had walked plenty in the past: she had walked for civil rights and to ban the bomb, for equal opportunities and to reclaim the night; she had walked against gunnings-down and blowings-up; she had walked to oppose cuts to health and education, to protest endless interventions and invasions and security council resolutions; there had been walks for peace, for full employment, for fuel and, of late, for pensions. She was the same age as Bob Dylan, for goodness sake, she felt like reminding Clinton, sitting there, on the edge of his seat awaiting her reply.

— It's very kind to consider me, she eventually said. Bill and me shared a lot of interests; but to be honest, hiking and golf were two things we did not have in common.

— Why not take some time to consider it, he asked and she realised how disappointed he was.

She reached across the iron mesh surface of the table and patted him swiftly on the back of his hand and said:

— I miss him, you know.

This remark prompted Clinton to straighten up in the seat.

— Oh. I know, he hastened to assure her. Of course you do. He has left such a gap.

— I mean, she explained. It would be difficult to join the club knowing he was no longer a part of it.

Changing the subject, she mentioned how she and Bill both shared a love for gardening and indicated the wall with the ladder up against it.

— We put that netting up this time last year, she pointed out. And now the Clematis has come loose.

She immediately regretted drawing attention to the ladder for Clinton expressed concern on health and safety grounds and offered to at least hold the bottom of the ladder for her. The image of her scaling the ladder in the faded pair of jeans she wore and Clinton having a view of her posterior amused and appalled her in equal measure.

— No need to worry: I've already been up and down it three or four times today, she lied.

She helped Clinton on with his back pack and escorted him back around to the front of the house.

— Watch you don't trip up on your laces, Clinton reminded her how she had merely slipped her feet back into the boots when she had sat down again to tea.

— Stay in touch, she told him and he went off assuring her he would.

It had been pleasant having the visit; yet also tiring, so she sat again on returning to the garden and, placing a palm against the pot, felt enough residual heat to persuade her to pour another cup of tea. Sipping this she sat and contemplated the garden.

— The garden never stops, she said aloud.

A soft breeze was enough to stir the errant strands of clematis and summon her. With a sigh, she inclined enough in her seat to knot the boot laces. She got to her feet and walked across the lawn to the ladder. She held it, as if by its lapels, and gave it a firm shake. Then she ascended four rungs, high enough to reach the loose tendrils.

Hawks

As she set about fastening and trapping the wayward vines and leafstalks again within the mesh that she and Bill had secured to the wall the previous year, she considered up close the tight knots and beads of buds that seemed suddenly to have proliferated all around her and this foretelling of an impending refulgence of flower felt suddenly very cruel and unkind, as did the whole bustle of nature, the buds and shoots and growth, the openings up and burstings forth and at that moment, perched as she was half way up the ladder, in mid air almost, the emptiness of widowhood hollowed her out and she clung to the rung in front of her, not in fear of falling but fearing rather that she would float off, blow away; inconsequential.